ABOUT THE AUTHOR

Regina Amollo was born in Kaberamaido in eastern Uga....
studied at Lwala St Mary's Girls School, Mt St Mary's Namagunga
Secondary School and Mulago School of Nursing, where she
qualified as a paediatric nurse.

Amollo's short story, *Those Days in Iganga* was published in *A
Woman's Voice,* an anothology of short stories published by
FEMRITE 1998. *A Season Of Mirth* is her first novel. She is
currently working in Soroti Hospital.

A SEASON OF MIRTH

Regina Amollo

FEMRITE PUBLICATIONS LIMITED
KAMPALA-UGANDA

FEMRITE Publications
P. O. Box 705 Kampala, Tel: 256-41-543943/077 743943
Email: femrite@infocom.co.ug
KAMPALA, Uganda

First published 1999
Reprinted 2003

Printed in Uganda by **Excel Graphics**

ISBN   9970 9010 6 0

ACKNOWLEDGEMENT

I wish to thank Mr Austin Ejiet of Makerere University for his valuable encouragement. I also want to thank Ayeta Anne Wangusa and Mary Karooro Okurut for the different roles they played to bring about the creation of this book.

DEDICATION

To my daughters Victoria Harriet and Veronica Lydia. And also to my father Esemu, and in memory of my mother Agnes, brothers John and Julius.

Chapter One

The day was breaking when Okanya got out of his grass-thatched house carrying a calabash of water. He was wearing a black pair of trousers, without a shirt. He went to the end of the courtyard and started washing his face. The morning air was very cold but he liked the way it caressed his naked upper body. The air was fresh from the previous day's rain. Dew hung heavily on the vegetation. A small wind rustled through the tree leaves, making the dew come down like rain. The whole place was again quiet until a bird flew overhead, singing. Its noise was followed by a cockcrow from Okanya's brother's home where smoke could already be seen wreathing skyward, lending the atmosphere a grey tint.

Okanya was about to go back to the house when he saw a man ride by on a bicycle. 'This is it then,' he said to himself as if he had just been waiting for the man to pass. He superstitiously believed that meeting a man first thing in the morning was a good omen. He hated meeting a woman first and quite often cancelled his journey when he did so, except if the female was a small girl. Small girls were not associated with bad luck. Okanya was going to the cattle market and felt that the day was going to be a good one.

"Assistant?" he called to his wife. There was no immediate reply. But he could hear the creaking of their old bed which meant that she was preparing to get up.

Abeso Maria was the name of Okanya's wife but to him she was 'assistant' in every way. He would call her 'Maria' only when he was drunk. He didn't know why he felt tender towards her only when he was drunk, but he did. Then he called her 'Maria' and felt good. Those occasions, however, were rare. And whenever he was in that mood, he would promise her gifts and see to it that he fulfilled his promise.

"Good morning, Dan!" Abeso greeted Okanya. She always used the shortened form of his name whenever she wanted to put him in a good mood, or to ask him for something. She did not want to go to the cattle market today and wanted him in good humour when she told him that.

Her husband, who stood facing her sitting on a low stool outside their house, was immediately suspicious that something was up. Ignoring her greeting, he demanded, "Are you not coming with me to the market?"

"Please forgive me."

"Forgive you for what?" Okanya asked, his good mood immediately deserting him.

"I am not feeling well," Abeso explained.

"What is the matter then?"

"I said that I am not feeling well, isn't that enough?"

"How can it be enough when I don't know if it is the head, the eye or the stomach which is paining you?"

"It is my head."

"I know it is a lie," Okanya said unsympathetically.

"You don't care whether I am sick or well. All you care about is using me as a beast to carry things for you. And what do I get from it all, a kilo of meat which is eaten by all of us!" Abeso was now sweating because she had, in her short speech, told Okanya that he was selfish, something she knew he could not stomach.

Okanya put the calabash of water down, and threateningly moved to where his wife was sitting. Sure that he was going to hit her, Abeso averted her face from him. Let him beat her if he wanted but she would not look at him while he was doing it. She sat still, steeled for the blows she knew must come. Okanya indeed felt tempted to slap her but restrained himself. He remembered when he had beaten her three years back and she had ran away to her parents' home. She had refused to come back for almost a year. He could not afford to

2

lose her again now. She was a good assistant in spite of her stubbornness. So he forced himself to cool down before he resumed in his normal voice, "You shouldn't say things like that, my dear." Abeso sighed with relief and he was pleased that he had frightened her. "Don't look scared, I am not going to beat you. What wrong have you done to force me to discipline you?" he went on soothingly. "You say that I am selfish but that is because you don't understand me. You always decide to ask me for things at the wrong time."

"How am I supposed to know when it is the right time?" Abeso asked him.

"I will tell you one day. But in the meantime, come and help me." He peeped at her still averted face and added, "Don't look as if I am going to eat you! Give me a smile. I want to go when there is no anger between us. It will help me to deal with customers better." He pulled the cloth she was covering herself with away and tickled her until she laughed. "You old rib!" he teased her, "I knew there was no headache. Why do women always say things indirectly?"

"I don't know," Abeso replied, rolling the bicycle out of the house. She stood it against a pole on the verandah and went back in the house to help him get the sack of groundnuts out. Each one got hold of one end of the sack but as they were going through the door, a nail caught Abeso's dress and she asked him to lower the sack to the ground. "What is the matter?" Okanya asked her. "I am already late as it is without you trying to delay me further."

"My dress is tearing," Abeso protested.

"Let the old thing go, who cares!"

"I care. Where will I get another dress from?"

"I will buy you another one."

"As if you mean what you say! I have stopped hoping for new clothes. But at least you can get me some thread to mend it, can't you?"

"Okay, okay, now can we lift the sack?" They put the sack astride the bicycle carrier and secured it with a rubber strip. Then Okanya went back in the house to put on his shirt while Abeso held the bicycle steady. A few minutes later, Okanya came out of the house donning a straw hat, rubber sandals and a second-hand short-sleeved shirt he

3

had bought from Kalaki market the previous Saturday. He felt very smart and ready to go. "Please don't forget the sewing thread," his wife reminded him. He nodded as he disappeared behind the old house which was once his late father's.

Chapter Two

After sweeping and putting her house in order, Abeso went to the kitchen and roused her daughters by kicking the door. "When are you going to get up? The sun is already up and you two are still sleeping!"

Like the main house, the kitchen was also grass-thatched and mud-walled. When she opened the door, the creaking woke the two girls who were sleeping in one bed in a corner of the single room.

Abeso had not come to greet her daughters. She wanted to go and see somebody, but had to apportion the housework between the girls before going. She went around the room to see what work needed doing. When she came to the pot of millet flour, she took off the cover and peeped inside. Then turned to Anaro saying, "Whose turn is it to cook today?"

"Mine, mother," Anaro answered, scrambling out of bed.

"Okay, you had better start early because I want us to have beans with potatoes for lunch. Your father has gone to the cattle market at Otuboi, let us hope that he will bring something nice for supper."

"Did you remind him about the pencil?" Ikiso asked. She had told her mother to tell Okanya to buy her a pencil because the one she had been using was used up. She was in P.7. at Lwala St. Mary's Primary School.

"What happened to your dress, mother?" Anaro asked, noticing the big hole in her mother's dress.

5

"Let mother answer me first," Ikiso said belligerently.

"Shut up, you! You are just a school kid and should keep quiet when grown ups are talking," Anaro hissed.

"You were once a school girl," her sister reminded her.

"Yes, and I learnt good manners."

"Where are they? What is the first one?"

"I don't see yours either. Mother is here, and you can't even get up to say good morning? What does that teacher with a big mouth teach you at school?"

"Don't abuse my teacher," Ikiso said tearfully. "Mother, Anaro is abusing my teacher."

"Don't start fighting now, children," Abeso told them.

"But is that teacher your brother? Why are you so concerned about him? No wonder they say you have a crush on him!"

"I don't, I don't. You are a liar, Anaro."

"Get up, you lazy girl," Anaro said, pulling the blanket away from Ikiso.

"Stop rowing, you two and listen to me," their mother intervened. "I am going to assign work to each of you to do during my absence. I am going across the road to see my sick aunt."

"Can I go with you, mother?" Ikiso asked.

"If you go, I will go too," Anaro jumped in.

"No one is coming with me. If all of us go, who will prepare lunch?" their mother asked. "You know what your father is like if he comes back and finds no lunch. What do you think he will do to me? Do you want him to beat me?"

"No," Anaro and Ikiso said together.

"Then be good girls and do what I tell you."

"Yes, mother, tell us," Anaro said. She loved her mother more than her father. She was older than Ikiso but had dropped out of school after P.7 for lack of school fees.

"Anaro, you will cook lunch of potatoes and beans as I told you. And you, Ikiso, collect water from the well and wash my *gomasi* for Mass to-morrow," Abeso said. "I have left soap in a basin with the *gomasi* outside our bedroom."

"Please, mother, ask her to wash my dress too," Anaro begged.

6

"I will not wash it. Don't you have hands?" Ikiso snarled.

"Can't you wash your own dress, Anaro?" Abeso asked, siding with her younger daughter.

"My work is heavier than hers. I will not clean the kitchen if she refuses to wash for me."

"That I will not allow, Anaro," her mother told her impatiently. "Food cooked in a dirty kitchen can never be good. Before you start cooking, take all the dirty utensils outside, cover all the food pots, remove the ash from the cooking place and sweep the kitchen. I dont want to hear you talk of cooking in a dirty kitchen. I am teaching you all this so that when you get married I will not be blamed for not bringing you up properly." She knew that Anaro was justified in complaining about having heavier work than her sister but Ikiso had a quick temper like her father and needed to be handled carefully. "Are you happy with what you are going to do, Ikiso?" she asked her.

"Yes, I think so," Ikiso replied.

"Will you do me a favour then and wash Anaro's dress?"

"If *you* ask me, mother, then I will do it."

"You are a good girl, Ikiso. I want to come home and find a clean kitchen and food ready, Anaro. I will be back about noon."

Satisfied that everything was all right between the girls, Abeso went to the house, got five shillings which she tied in one corner of her handkerchief, pushed it inside her brassier and set off on her journey. Her destination was the home of an old woman called Lakeri, who lived across the road.

She had met Lakeri in a market near her home when she had ran away after Okanya beat her mercilessly. The old woman had then advised her to go back to her husband and look after her children. "Men are like wild animals. If you run away from them, they will come after you again. What you do, my daughter, is tame them and I can help you do that if you come to my house."

Abeso had accordingly gone to Lakeri's house who had given her some dry leaf as a talisman to keep on herself. If Abeso noticed any improvement in her husband's treatment of her, she was to go back and report. Since coming back from her parents' home, Abeso thought that there had surely been some change in Okanya! For example this morning, the old Okanya would have beaten her senseless for refusing to go to the market with him. So it must have been the leaf from the old woman which had saved her from that beating, and many others before, she concluded.

As she walked quickly along the footpath, for she wanted to be back before her husband came from the market, she was assailed by hot humid air. It might rain, she thought, looking up at the large white clouds which broke the blue sky in parts.

Abeso walked silently along the footpath which would soon meet with the main road. She was going eastwards, which meant facing the sun but it was not yet hot. She was in fact enjoying the warmth it gave. She was also admiring the vegetation which was green and lush after the rain of the previous night. Black ants flew everywhere, attracting the attention of birds which went after them, enjoying a good breakfast. She saw many people on the main road walking in the direction of Otuboi where the cattle market was being held that day. Men were carrying simsim, fresh and dry fish, groundnuts and other commodities on bicycles while women on foot, carried their loads on their heads.

After Abeso crossed the road, she saw Molly, her brother's wife. "Good morning?" Molly greeted her. "Are you not going to the market today?"

"Good morning, my dear. No, I am not going to the market today. I am not feeling well," Abeso lied.

"I am sorry to hear that," Molly said sympathetically.

"It is only a headache." Molly was easy to deceive, unlike Okanya who would ask you all sorts of questions as if he was a doctor.

"Let me hurry, Otuboi is still far," Molly said.

"You can come back in a lorry."

"That is if I get money from this millet."

"They will buy it, especially these Karimojong traders," Abeso told her and Molly hurried away.

Abeso went straight on and when she reached an acacia tree, she turned right. As she approached the compound, a dog barked and Lakeri came out to see who the intruder was.

"Come on, my daughter," she invited. "That dog does not bite.

8

Hush, Ajegere," she soothed the dog which had continued to bark. It went and lay in front of the main house which faced Lakeri's medium sized one.

Lakeri and Abeso entered the house. "I was afraid that I might not find you in but I came all the same," Abeso said.

"Did you meet anyone on your way?"

"No," Abeso lied.

"That in itself is a good sign."

"I thought that if one met a man, then the journey would be good?" Abeso asked.

"Not every man has a lucky face and not everyone is the same," Lakeri told her. "For example, if I meet a man, it means bad luck."

"But Okanya says that man is good luck to everybody."

"No, that is a lie. When a couple's first born is a girl, it means good luck to them. So how can the same female turn out to be bad luck?" Lakeri reasoned.

"But how come our first born is a girl and all has not been well with us?" Abeso asked puzzled.

"How do you know he had no child outside already?" Lakeri asked her. "But don't let that worry you, my daughter. By the way," she added lowering her voice, "how is he now? Has his temper improved?" Abeso looked at the old woman with awe, wondering how she could have known that Okanya had a child outside. Should she tell her the truth about Okanya's changed temper? But she wanted another leaf to make him buy her new clothes. After thinking about it, she decided not to tell the whole truth and said, "He is a bit better. This morning I refused to carry groundnuts to the cattle market and although I feared that he would beat me, he didn't," she confessed and felt the same kind of relief she used to feel after confessing to a priest. That was many years ago. She had married Okanya traditionally and the priest had stopped her from going for confession and receiving Holy Communion.

"That is good but not enough. You have to please your husband and obey him. You have to welcome him back with a smile and cook good food for him. Do you hear that, my daughter?"

9

"But how can I smile to him when he is too drunk to notice my smile when he comes back?" Abeso wondered.

"Does he drink a lot?"

"Yes, sometimes."

"I will give you another leaf. A man who drinks too much is no good and can sometimes beat you without being aware of what he is doing."

"What you say, grandmother, is true. The last time he beat me, he was too drunk to know what he was doing," Abeso concurred.

"Yes, I remember. Why didn't that brother of his help you? I could hear your call for help, it was heart-rending."

"He locked me in the bedroom. The children screamed and many people came but could do nothing. Ocen threatened to set the house on fire all to no avail. Eventually they broke the door and rescued me but by then I was blind and unconscious. If *you* had not advised me to return, with the help of this leaf, I would not have gone back to him. He would have received his cows back instead."

"I know how you feel but don't be bitter about it. I will help you and you will be all right," the old woman promised.

"I hope it will continue that way," Abeso said. When she remembered that beating, tears pricked her eyes. He had beaten her with the intention of killing her. How could she ever forgive him that! He was lucky those children saved his home from collapsing. Where would he find another woman who worked like her?

She looked around her. Near the door stood two big water pots covered with old enamel plates. There was a smaller, third pot next to the other two, turned upside down. Lakeri's wooden bed, covered with a mosquito net, which had turned greyish due to smoke, stood in one corner of the house. Lakeri used her one room as kitchen, bedroom and visitors' reception room.

The fireplace was some two yards away from her bed and was always smouldering because she could not afford matches. So there was always a pile of wood on the ready to keep the fire from going out. And as a result of the constant smoke, the roof of the house had turned black with soot. Under the bed, a wooden box, dark with age, could be seen.

Lakeri went to the foot of the bed where a big pot stood. She opened it, poured two calabashes of water in it and put it on the fire to boil as she muttered to herself something like 'Let my daughter drink the remainder. I knew someone was coming because my eyelid kept twitching. It was telling me my daughter was coming. That is why I kept a little beer'. She went outside and came back with a small pot and a straw tube used for drinking millet beer.

"You will make me drunk so early in the morning," Abeso said as the old woman put a small pot in front of her.

"It is not much," Lakeri said. She then got a calabash which was hanging over the fireplace and got beer from the pot at the foot of the bed and poured it in the small pot, leaving a little in the calabash for Abeso to test. Abeso made the sign of the cross and drank. When she made a face at the bitter taste, the old woman looked pleased. She always made strong stuff.

"It is very nice," Abeso said, by way of compliment. "I hope I won't get drunk and forget what brought me."

"I will not allow you to forget."

"I am just joking. In fact, I want to leave here around eleven so that I can be home before Okanya comes back."

"You will go, don't worry. Now pull," Lakeri added, handing Abeso a straw tube after sprinkling some beer down for the ancestral spirits.

"Add some hot water. It is so cold," Abeso said.

"Then drink so that there is more room for water," Lakeri advised her. Abeso drank, and then handed the pot back to Lakeri. They drank in turns because they were using one straw. After sometime, Lakeri asked, "My daughter, tell me why you were beaten last time."

"It was just a simple matter, grandmother. Okanya said that he met someone who told him that he had seen Anaro, my eldest daughter, at the *okembo* dance at Okwapa's home sometime back. He asked me what I was doing when Anaro escaped to go to the dance and I told him that I was sleeping. He did not believe it. So that was why he started beating me."

"Does he not allow Anaro to attend dances?"

"He would not hear of it."

"Why, doesn't he want cows?"

11

"He wants them very much, that is why he is strict with the girls."

"What! Does he think men will meet them in your your compound?"

"I don't know. But he shouldn't blame me when they escape to go to dances."

"But beating you, suppose he disfigured you, what then?"

"I don't know what to do, that is why I have come to you for help."

"Do you have two shillings?"

"I have a five shillings note."

"I will change it," kakeri said and went to the foot of the bed where she kept her money in a hole. She got it out and rubbed it between her hands to remove the dust and then got a piece of cloth from her gourd and went back to Abeso.

She untied the note of the cloth with her teeth and handed Abeso some strange sustance saying, "Here is the medicine." Abeso took it, wondering what it could be. But if it could change Okanya from a bull to a lamb, that is all that matters, she thought to herself.

"Put a little in his food and the rest in his water," the old woman directed. "You will be happy with him until the end of your days. Good luck!"

Abeso took the medicine wrapped in a brownish paper with her left-hand. She feared to use her right-hand in case she forgot to wash before eating but Lakeri chided her saying, "Don't ever use your left-hand to receive medicine. This medicine is harmless," she added, licking a bit of it. "Now, when you leave, don't say goodbye and don't look behind. Keep the medicine outside your bedroom and make it work even better by trying to be good. God will help you."

"I think I better go now. It is getting late," Abeso said and left without saying goodbye.

Chapter Three

"Oh Bikira Maria, look! Come and see, Anaro," Ikiso said.

"What is it?"

"Do you see that heap?"

"Is that all? I thought you were calling me for something terrible."

"It is terrible. Does mother think I can finish this heap?"

"You are always complaining, Ikiso. It is not good."

"Then will you help me?"

"If you think going to dig up potatoes is easy, then I will help you. Oh," Anaro said, looking excited, "there is a dance at Okwapa's tonight. Lilly told me." Lilly was a girl of Anaro's age who was staying with her aunt across the road.

"I want also to go," Ikiso said.

"If we both go, father will find out."

"But supposing he wants you?" Ikiso pointd out.

"I will not go until he is asleep."

"He went to the cattle market, he is sure to pass somewhere to drink and come back late."

"I will still go. The dance stops at 5 a.m. but I will come back before that of course." Then it occurred to her that the best way to buy Ikiso's cooperation was to help her with the washing. "Let's do it this way, you put the beans on the fire and sweep the kitchen while I run to get the potatoes. I will be back in no time."

Anaro got a hoe and an old basket and ran to the garden. The soil was soft, so the potatoes were easy to dig out. Unfortunately, in her haste, she cut her toe with the hoe and cried out in pain. But there was nobody to hear her except a herdsman who was grazing his cattle in an old sorgham garden. She gathered her potatoes in the basket, put the load on her head and limped back home.

"You are already back, did you run?" Ikiso asked.

"My legs are long, can't you see?"

"But you are sweating?"

"You are so childish, Ikiso, do you think digging, carrying this basket and walking in that hot sun a joke?" Anaro retorted irritably because her toe was hurting. "Get me some water to wash my foot."

"Ai, you cut your toe! How did you do it?"

"I just cut it. Get some water and stop talking nonsense." The toe had started throbbing and it seemed to her as if the pain was coming right from the heart. She washed both feet. "Do you know where mother keeps her aspirin?" Ikiso went to check in their parents' room but she came back to report that the room was locked. "Then boil some hot water for me. I think it works in the same way as aspirin because whenever I have a heavy cold or a headache, mother uses hot water."

So Anaro applied some hot water to the wound and immediately felt some relief. "Will you go to the dance?" Ikiso asked.

"Why not? It will be all right, in fact I don't feel the pain now after using the hot water. Let's go to the well for some water. But add more water to the food and don't forget to close the door."

At the well, they met Lilly, her friend. "Dear me, what happened to you?" Lilly asked, looking at the toe.

"It is the trick our old hoe likes to play on us."

"Will you be able to come to the dance?"

"Of course I will. I can't miss it for the world."

"I will come for you as arranged then," Lilly said.

"Of course. But don't forget to come stealthily."

"I won't. What are you going to do now?"

"I am going to wash clothes. Have you forgotten that tomorrow is Sunday?" Anaro remarked. They saw some village women coming and after arranging when to meet, hurriedly said goodbye and parted.

Anaro and her sister put some water in the kitchen and kept some under the tree in front of the house for washing clothes. They repeated the trip to the well four times and then Anaro entered the granary to get some unshelled groundnuts.

Okanya had four big granaries. They had umbrella-like tops and rested on four big stones. Anaro used a forked piece of log which stood against the granary and acted as a ladder. She used this to climb the one in which groundnuts were kept. She gave the groundnuts to Ikiso to shell and roast while she washed clothes. "But I will burn them," Ikiso protested after she had finished shelling.

"Okay, you put these clothes up to dry and I will roast the groundnuts." After that she swept the compound because their mother had told them she wanted to come back to a clean home. When the food was ready, Ikiso wanted to eat but Anaro refused, saying they would wait for their mother to come back. She always insisted on waiting for their mother to come back from wherever she had gone but this day, Ikiso felt particularly hungry.

"I say, can't we eat? Mother will eat with father," she pleaded but Anaro was adamant. So she went outside and came back with a raw potato which she intended to roast in the fireplace but as soon as she bent down to put it in, her sister pulled her up by the ears so hard that she started to cry. "I will tell father everything today," she threatened through her tears. "I will tell him about the boy who came here last Sunday and I will not answer for you tonight when he calls you during your absence."

She went on crying, using her skirt to wipe her running nose. Her ear felt as if it were on fire and her stomach was rumbling. Let her mother come and see how Anaro was mistreating her.

Anaro herself was infuriated with Ikiso's threat to reveal her secrets. If she dared carry out her threat, she would regret it, she vowed and was about to tell Ikiso as much when she looked behind and saw their mother. "Mother, welcome back."

"Mother, Anaro has been beating me," Ikiso put in quickly. She was not going to give Anaro a chance to escape.

"What happened?" Abeso asked, looking from Ikiso's tearful face to Anaro.

15

"She refused to let us eat and when I tried to roast a potato, she pulled my ears. They are still paining up to now." She released fresh tears as she tenderly touched her ear.

"And Anaro? Tell me what happened."

"Ikiso wanted us to eat at ten, so I refused."

"She is lying, it was twelve thirty."

"I am not. And I just touched her ear, mother, and she started wailing. She was crying for food and not because I hurt her," Anaro argued.

"If the food was ready, why didn't you give it to her? Food is not for hoading, is it?" Her mother wanted to know but Anaro had no answer. Ikiso looked triumphant. But then her mother turned to her and said, "And you, Ikiso, after this year, you will be joining boarding school. There they don't eat anything between breakfast and lunch; so you must learn to control your hunger." Now it was Ikiso's turn to look down and Anaro's to look pleased.

"Take the mat under the tree," Anaro ordered Ikiso. She served the food and they sat in a circle and ate from the same dish.

****

Okanya was heavy at heart when he left home that morning. However good you are to women, he said to himself, it is just a waste of time. I buy her meat every week; she has two dresses; two *gomas;* she sleeps on a mattress, covers herself with sheets and a blanket, but what thanks do I get? When I first met her, she had only one dress and used to sleep on a cow-hide, aren't women funny! They live in the present only; forget the past, the future either doesn't exist for them or they leave it entirely to the men to take care of.

Okanya was cycling slowly as these thoughts ran through his mind. The path was narrow and the dew hung heavily on the grass. The cold air made him chilly so that he had to wipe his running nose on his shirtsleeve from time to time. On the murram road he met a man going in the same direction and the two travelled together. He felt happier and assured of a good day.

The market was already full even at that early hour when Okanya

16

got there. Everbody was busy talking as they arranged their merchandise for sale. Okanya sat near his friend Orace who was also selling groundnuts.

One side of the market was turned into a large pen for cows, goats and sheep. It had one entrance at which the *gombolola* chief sat issuing receipts.

Next to this animal shed was the secondhand clothes section where traders were busy displaying them. Not far from there, other clothes sellers, mainly women, were also busy hanging them up on poles.

For sale in the market were also other goods like food stuffs, both dry and fresh, medicines of all types with the touts blaring their qualities on loud speakers as if they wanted the whole world to hear.

"Have you heard?" Okanya asked his friend, grinning with amusement because it was rumoured that Orace had suffered from G.C once.

"All that nonsense is for young ones. It has nothing to do with an old man like me," Orace said, wishing to drop the subject. His rescue came in the form of a girl wishing to buy groundnuts. He welcomed her quickly, "Maria, or is it Rose?" he called out with relief. "Come and buy some groundnuts. They go well with that fish you bought."

"Who said I am Maria?" the girl retorted, annoyed.

"Leave that *musei* if he is disturbing you," Okanya quickly jumped in.

"That man has a daughter as big as your elder sister, so don't let him confuse you," Orace hit back at Okanya.

"I don't want to confuse her, I only want to serve her as quickly as possible so that she can go." The girl listened to the two men fighting over her and was uncertain whom to buy from. Finally, she decided to buy one shilling's worth of groundnuts from each one of them.

"You are a wise girl. I wish I had a son," Okanya said.

"I have one, my daughter," Orace said and the girl laughed at the idea and left them.

They were settling down to more business of selling when there was a commotion from the animal section. Apparently there was an old man who was failing to control his cow.

"Has he no son?" Orace wondered.

17

"You never think of anything but sons," Okanya commented, pretending to be bored with the subject. He had no son and did not find the subject of sons amusing. His wife was thirty three years old but since the birth of Ikiso, who was thirteen years old, he had stopped to hope for another child. Let him gloat about his sons, he thought angrily, I will show them one day that a girl can be better than a boy in more than one way. Boys are parasites; you educate them, look after them, marry them wives... if you are lucky, one might become a policeman and make you feel happy, but only for a short time. He goes to Kampala, leaving you alone, with no one to relieve your wife of cooking in the kitchen. After three years, you get a letter telling you that your son has two children, a boy and a girl named after you both. The wife is happy and starts pounding simsim and groundnuts, and tying bundles of white ants which she keeps hanging over the fireplace. She does all this in April for a son who is not expected until December.

The son and his family come with presents for his family, they spend leave at home. When the parents are beginning to enjoy the company of their grandchildren, the son declares his intention of going back to Kampala, refusing to part with his family. I prefer a daughter, Okanya consoled himself. Of course it is good to have a son, he went on musing to himself, but he would not allow people like Orace to dip their fingers in his wound.

"I am going to buy something for my people, will you please look after my things?" he asked Orace.

"Come back quickly because I want to eat something before I go," his friend said.

"I thought we were going together?"

Okanya bought fish, remembered the thread Abeso wanted and bought it too. He then went to a small restaurant behind the market, where he ate meat and millet bread. He remembered his wife saying, 'The reward I get for carrying goods for you is just one kilo of meat which is eaten by everybody. Did she want to eat it alone?

He almost burst out laughing. Okay, I will get her something she will not have to share with everybody, he decided and bought her a pair of slippers. And then he decided to buy his daughters slippers too. A smart daughter brings a smart son-in-law, he told himself. Then he bought medicines like aspirin, chloroquine and cough mixture and was now ready to go home.

"I say, you are a real businessman ," he said to Orace when he went back and saw two empty sacks in front of him.

"As soon as you left, they dropped on me like locusts," Orace said.

"I hope they didn't cheat you?"

"I am too clever for them. Let me go and put something in my stomach too."

"Then hurry. See those clouds over there? They look watery to me," Okanya said as he surveyed the sky.

Chapter Four

They rolled their bicycles carefuly until they reached the road. Orace was about to cross the road when an urgent alarm from a lorry full of people stopped him.

"You don't seem to love your life," Okanya said to him.

"I do very much," Orace replied nervously. He had had a narrow escape.

"On a day like this, you cannot be too careful on this road," Okanya remarked. "You have to check each direction several times before you dare to cross."

"I wonder where that lorry is taking all those people."

"Those are Langis from Dokolo, Lira, Abako, and so on. This cattle market collects so many people. Those selling old and new clothes are from Kenya, Iganga, Jinja and Kaliro," Okanya told him.

"How do you know all that?" Orace asked. They were riding uphill and Okanya found talking difficult, so he just grunted, "I know," and the two rode in silence.

As they neared their village, they started looking for signs of a home with local brew. This was usually achieved by planting a stick or two in the middle of the path leading to the home selling the beer.

Half a mile from Orace's home, they found one and branched off. The home belonged to Esemu and his wife Agenesi, a cheerful elderly woman. They were warmly welcomed and given chairs under a tree facing the kitchen. "How was the cattle market?" Esemu asked, getting himself a chair and joining them.

"Full as usual. Those Bantus from Iganga and Kaliro flock here in numbers," Okanya said.

"I think things here are cheap, that is why they keep coming," Esemu said. "Whereas a cow is between one and five thousand here, I hear it costs six thousand shillings there," he added. Then he called to his wife to bring the visitors something.

"You will have to wait, the water is not ready," Agenesi said from the kitchen.

"Why didn't you go to the market today?" Okanya asked Esemu.

"I was busy ploughing my cotton garden. This year poll tax is going to be increased, I know," Esemu said, worried.

"I know you are right. I will stop going to the cattle market too to prepare my garden."

Agenesi brought a medium sized pot of beer and put it down. Each mug, which was approximately half a litre, cost one shilling.

"How much should I pour for you?" she asked the two men.

Orace looked at his friend questioningly before he said, "We shall drink for two shillings." Agenesi looked at Okanya who nodded and said, "Yes, do as he says." When Agenesi was about to leave, her husband asked, "What about me? Give me some too. I have to talk with my brothers while we are still alive." Agenesi hesitated: if she gave him beer now, he would keep demanding for more as more drinkers came. Sometimes she felt like pouring a whole pot of beer on his head but restrained herself. She now added two more mugs in the calabash and Orace applauded her as a good wife. Hot water and straw tubes were brought and the men began to drink, after each had spat the first mouthful out on the ground.

The men discussed the cattle market as they drank and laughed loudly at some of the funny episodes which often took place, like the old man whose cattle had caused pandemonium that morning. They asked for more hot water and Agenesi brought it and then it was time to pay up.

"I have come," Agenesi said. The meaning was clear to everybody. Okanya dipped his hand into his pocket and gave Agenesi two shillings.

"And you?" she said, shifting her gaze to Orace. She could see that he was drunk; his eyes had a glazed look. "I want to go," she told him.

"Where are you going?" Orace asked drunkenly. "I have a fifty shillings note here." He touched his pocket. "I will change it and then I will bring your money to-morrow."

"I want my money now, Orace, so stop joking with me. When you left the cattle market, you knew you were going to drink, so why didn't you change it?" Agenesi asked, annoyed. Esemu and Okanya looked on in silence at first and then the latter said, "Stop behaving like a fool, Orace."

"Do you hear that, Esemu? That good-for-nothing man is calling me a fool," Orace complained.

"Give the woman her money then," Okanya said, looking dangerously at Orace. "If you have no change, I will change it for you." Orace did not reply; he did not like the way things were going since his aim was to postpone payment for the drink until a later date. Why is Okanya concerning himself with the matter, anyway, he wondered, feeling furious. Let him try anything and I will show him that I am Orace, son of Elau.

"Bring out the money," Okanya persisted, putting out his hand.

"Do I have your money?" Orace asked, looking aggressive.

"I am only trying to help you with change so that you can pay the woman."

"Has she no mouth to speak for herself?"

"Don't embarrass me, Orace," Okanya begged.

"In what way? Don't talk to me as if I were your son," Orace said, looking boldly at him. Okanya felt hurt by the reference to a son. He bunched his hand into a fist and got up and socked Orace on the face. He raised his chair and was about to bring it down on Orace's head when Esemu intervened, "Please, brother, don't fight." He removed the chair from Okanya and put it down. Orace had recovered from the shock and was rubbing his chin tenderly and breathing hard. He staggered towards Okanya with murderous rage but again Esemu intervened saying, "What is it, brothers? Did you two quarrel on the way? Surely you cannot be fighting because of the money!"

"Esemu has saved you," Orace said, pointing a finger at Okanya. "I would have shown you today that I am Orace, son of Elau."

"My father is dead but he knows that I am a son worth calling a son, not like some people with thieves for sons," Okanya said.

"Are you insulting me?" Orace asked, advancing towards Okanya again but Esemu held him back.

"You know your sons are thieves. They must have inherited the trade from you."

"What have I stolen from you?"

"Do you have to steal from me to be a thief? What about the woman's two shillings? Only two shillings!" Okanya remarked.

"A man who cannot produce a son has nothing to be proud of," Orace said stingingly.

"Just you wait and see. You will one day wish you had more daughters than sons," Okanya said, refusing to be angered.

"My son is a policeman," Orace boasted. "What about you? Nothing."

"Oh that one who cannot even buy you a pair of trousers! You are always in shorts like a schoolboy."

"But what have your daughters done for you?"

"I said wait and you will see. My daughters will one day bring me something your sons will never dream of doing for you."

"What can they bring you except cows?"

"Narrow-minded fool, he thinks of nothing else but cows!"

"Stop abusing me. Look at your head! Your mother must have suffered pushing it out."

"Don't bring in my mother or I will make you see stars again."

"Try and you will never stop regretting it!"

"Brothers, brothers, please, let us sit down and discuss this problem quietly," Esemu stepped in.

Paying no heed to him, Orace continued addressing Okanya, "You think you are important?"

"Yes. And to show that I am a gentleman too, here, Agenesi, take your money. I am the one who brought this cheat here," Okanya said, giving Agenesi a five shilling note.

"Bring back the beer," Esemu said and sat down. The others followed his example. When Agenesi brought back the beer, Orace gave her a ten shilling note saying, "Wife, forgive the son of Elau.

23

Please, don't see me in poor light. This gentleman here," he added, pointing to Okanya, "interfered so much, making me lose my temper. And now, brother," Orace continued, turning to Esemu, "shake hands to show that there was no ill-feeling meant."

"And none taken," Esemu assured him, shaking his hand.

"That is the spirit. Shake mine too," said Okanya.

"Yeah, brother, forget what I said and let us start afresh. To begin with - beer. Agenesi, our wife, where are you?" When Agenesi came, he told her, "I don't need any of the balance from that ten shilling note. It is beer we need now to clear the confusion from our minds. Not so , brothers?" he asked. The other two agreed with him. He then took a packet of crown bird cigarettes and offered it around, before he called for fire. Agenesi came back with a piece of burning wood from which the cigarettes were lit. She also offered Okanya his money back since Orace had settled his bill but he refused it saying they were still drinking.

"That is the spirit," Orace said, clapping his hands.

"I am happy to have two understanding friends," Esemu said. "If it had been Edila, he would never have acceded to a reconciliation."

"Where is he these days?" Okanya asked.

"I hear he got a job as a gatekeeper at a spinning mill in Lira," Orace said.

"Oh that boy could drink!" Esemu remarked.

"If he has continued his drinking, I can't see him lasting there," Okanya observed. "A gatekeeper has to be fully awake when on duty at night."

Edila was the son of Orace's neighbour who was well-known as a trouble-maker. He used to worry his old father so much that most of the time the old man would stay awake, waiting to be called in to calm tempers aroused by him.

After discussing Edila, they discussed the weather and then farming, especially the group farming scheme in Lwala.

"Where are we going to plant cotton this year?" Esemu wondered.

"I heard they are giving us gardens for group farming in Lwala. The chief has found a large piece somewhere there," Okanya answered.

"I was trying to prepare my garden here. If I get one there, then I will have to plant millet in this one," Esemu said.

24

"That is it, you can plant anything anywhere, but not cotton, because the government wants us to do group farming to make it easier for them to see how much a county or a district has produced," Orace remarked.

"You are behind the news," Okanya said. "The meaning of group farming is to find out easily who has not planted cotton."

"I don't think so," Esemu argued. "I think it helps the Agricultural field workers when they come to see crops and to advise us."

"Maybe," Okanya conceded.

"But imagine going to Lwala, almost two miles away to dig!" Orace said.

"What can you do? If it is Lwala, it must be Lwala, nobody will change it," Okanya said.

"Water please," Esemu called. Hot water was brought. More people came and the beer pot grew bigger. They drank until late. At around six Okanya left Esemu's home for his own. Orace remained behind. He was the type to see everything to the end! Okanya left without saying 'good-bye' to the host. When he got up, he discovered that he was drunk, so he just rolled away his bicycle. It was getting dark. Cows were coming back home and birds were singing good night to their friends. By the time Okanya joined the main road he felt steady enough to ride his bicycle. He rode for a while, then disembarked when he felt dizzy and nauseous. He remembered the fish in the bag and hoped his wife had cooked something else for supper. Old tunes came to his head and he started singing, softly at first, then more loudly as he neared his home.

Chapter Five

The afternoon wore on. Wind blew a lot, scattering the clouds. It was 5 p.m but there was no sign of her husband yet. He must be drinking somewhere along the road, Abeso thought. Anyway, she was not worried about him. It was her chance to give him what Lakeri had given. But something must be done about supper.

"Ikiso, Ikiso," she called. Ikiso did not answer but just presented herself in the doorway. "Where is your sister?"

"Lilly is plaiting her hair!"

" Tell her I am calling her," Abeso said and continued tidying the house.

"Why did mother call you "Anaro asked her sister.

"She wants to see you," Ikiso said and sat down near Lilly, who was kneeling behind Anaro, plaiting hair. Anaro sat on a mat with her legs stretched before her.

"Let me go, Lilly, and hear why I am wanted," Anaro said.

"Wait a minute; let me finish this line then you can go," Lilly said and plaited quickly.

Only half of Anaro's head was finished. The head would resemble a cotton field when done. Lilly made straight lines from the front of the head to the back. This fashion was known as *"kiswahili."*

"How much food is left? I mean sauce?" Abeso asked Anaro.

"Not much, I left some for father."

"Your father has not yet come back. I expected he would bring us something for supper but it seems he is drinking beer somewhere.

People left the cattle market long ago, I know."

"What do you want me to do?" Anaro asked.

"I want you to get more groundnuts so that we can have groundnut sauce for supper."

"There is already pounded groundnuts, mother. I did not use all this morning."

"That is good then. I will do the rest, go and finish plaiting your hair," she said looking her daughter up and down admiringly. Anaro is becoming a girl these days, she thought. It was true Anaro was turning into a beautiful girl. Tall, with black hair and a natural gap between her front upper teeth which made people want her to smile all the time.

After Lilly had finished plaiting her hair, she escorted her up to the main road. "When will you come back?" Anaro asked.

"I will come back at around nine."

"Make it ten. You know my father is not yet back."

"No, don't worry, even if I come at nine, we will be in the kitchen and I will wait for you."

"Okay. You know how to come, no noise. Do you know those who are going for the dance, I mean girls?" Anaro asked.

"Of course those girls from Lwala, Kadie and Kalaki will come. Even Joseph is going."

"But that one is in Kampala?"

"No, he came back today by *Saa-Mbaya* bus."

"Oh!"

"Yes, put on your best."

"I can't, my best dress is for Sunday."

"Anyway, that is all right. After all, it is at night, who will see what one has put on?"

"Bye for now," Anaro said and ran back home. They had supper and went to bed. Their mother took their father's supper to their room. She put his food on a small table and prepared bathing water in a basin. She was pleased that her husband never used hot water. She could not imagine warming water at night when he came back late! She did everything Lakeri had told her and lay on the bed awake, waiting for her man. She was starting to doze off when she heard him, as usual, introducing himself to the village as though he were a stranger.

27

Okanya was singing but the song was full of O-o-o-o-o. One could just hear the O's but no words. After the song, he would address an imaginary audience. Abeso heard him saying "Who is there? The son of the earth is here, son of the lion, Okanya, the light of the village." Pause, then in a rising voice he sang:

"*O—o—o*
My dear—O
The work is finished—O come home and till the land—O—
Your father gave it to you—O
And your grandfather gave your father—O so my dear come back!
Yes! No! We don't want thieves, nor wizards."

Okanya was nearing home.

It was dark now but he knew the road well. When he passed his father's house he said, "Rest in peace - amen." Okanya reached his compound. There was light in his house. He knew his wife was waiting for him.

Yes, such is my wife, he told himself. He felt pleased. "Mother, mother, your son is back, well and sound," Okanya called, standing in the compound. Abeso heard him and smiled to herself. She got out of bed and took the kerosene lamp with her to the sitting room. She wrapped a sheet around herself then she opened the door. It was dark outside. Her eyes were not accustomed yet to the darkness.

"Mother, I am here," Okanya said, feeling much love for the woman.

"Here, hold the bicycle, my bladder is bursting." Okanya said and went behind the house to pass urine. He came back, then went in and sat down, took off the straw hat, shirt and sandals. Abeso sat near the bedroom door watching him.

"Come, my dear, is there water? I need a bath badly, I feel sticky," he said, looking around as though taking a quick inventory of his belongings. The room was smart. Water pots were all covered with plates, his few chairs were well arranged, the only table he had, stood in the middle of the room. Plates on it had his food. He felt like drinking water and told his wife, "Bring me some water, mother, my assistant," his said, his gaze lingering on her. She avoided his gaze. He was behaving like a man in love today. She gave him water, then she

28

carried a basinful of water outside. She put it in front of the house. No need to take it to the bathroom. It was pitch dark. Okanya took a bath and went inside, leaving the basin outside. Abeso took it in and she gave him food. He ate in silence, then he started hiccuping.

"Who is talking about me now?" Okanya asked.

"Try to call their names," Abeso advised. She was worried. Could it be Lakeri's medicine? She hoped nothing serious would happen. "This must be that fool Orace—hiccough—Esemu—hiccup— Agenesi—hiccup," Okanya counted and called many names but the hiccup persisted. It was locally believed that when one called the name of the person talking about one at that time, the hiccough would stop.

But Okanya tried in vain. "Give me water to drink—hicough.. It is drying my throat—hiccup." Okanya drank deeply. While he was drinking the hiccup stopped. He drank more water and as a result he felt bad. He wanted to vomit. Why did he drink so much water? He was unable to continue with eating, so he pushed the plates away and got up. He went straight to bed and slept with the pair of trousers on. Abeso prayed nothing serious would happen.

Chapter Six

K ok, kok, kok," Lilly knocked at the kitchen door where Anaro and her sister slept.

"Who are you?" Anaro asked in a whisper. She was standing near the door. It was good to ask just to make sure in case it was their father. But no, he must be asleep by now. It is a good thing he is drunk, he will sleep soundly."

"It is me, Lilly."

"Oh! Forgive me, I had to make sure," Anaro said and opened the door very slowly. But despite the caution, the old tin door creaked loudly.

"You don't know how to open," Lilly whispered. "You do it quickly like this and it will sometimes make no noise," Lilly instructed swinging the door shut. It worked splendidly. It made noise but not much. "Now, are you ready?"

"I don't know if he is asleep," Anaro said and just then, they heard the door of the other house opening. They stiffened with fright. Lilly hurried to hide under the only bed in the house. Anaro went back to bed and covered herself. Her heart was beating so fast that she found herself releasing her breath in bits. Lilly worsened the situation by kicking the saucepan as she tried to settle under the bed. The noise it made sounded too loud in the quiet house. They waited for the worst. They expected Okanya at any moment. But nothing happened. Okanya had gone out to pass urine. He went back and closed the door behind him. The girls heard the door close shut and breathed normally again.

"E-eh! That was too close," Lilly said, emerging from under the bed.

"It is okay. Now he will not come to ask for me," Anaro said.

"How do you know?" Lilly asked.

"Usually he checks on me first time he comes out," Anaro assured her friend.

"Inform Ikiso that we are going," Lilly said.

"Ikiso! Ikiso!" Anaro shook her sister gently. "Ikiso! This child can be annoying sometimes: she is fast asleep," Anaro said and lifted Ikiso's head.

"Leave me alone," Ikiso said in a voice full of sleep.

"Listen, Ikiso," Anaro shook her. "Are you listening?"

"Yes."

"When father, calls answer as usual, okay?"

"Yes," Ikiso answered.

"And don't forget to open when I knock, Ikiso, are you listening?" Anaro asked.

"Yes," Ikiso said.

"Come and lock the door. Lilly, let us go," Anaro said and they left.

It was very dark outside. They held their hands as they went along the small foot path that led to the main road. Lilly's Aunt's home was somewhere across this very road. The road stretched northward. When one followed it northwards, one reached Lwala Mission and Lwala shops, where there was a market every Wednesday. Then it continued to Otuboi and other places. Anaro and her friend went southwards, towards Kalaki. It was around 9.30 p.m. The world was asleep; there was a frightening quietness all around. A dog barked from the neighbouring village and the girls felt better. Someone was also moving about, could be to the dance. People laughed from behind them, boys and girls.

"Those are Lwala girls," Lilly said softly.

"Those girls can't miss any dance, even if the dance is at Kalaki," Anaro remarked.

"Where are we branching off? Not here?" Lilly saked.

"Yes, this is it. I know it because of that tree." It was a *Kingur* tree at the left side of the road. It looked twice its size because of the darkness. The girls could just make out its outline. Okwapa, son of Emou was the one holding this dance. His home was just a short distance away from the road. So when Anaro and her friend left the main road, they could hear voices of people coming from Okwapa's home. Sweet music flowed towards them. It was a *Kiswahili* record playing and it was called *Dada Asha*.

As they came closer to the home, the music grew louder. The sky was clear. Stars winked mischievously down at them. Some were big and bright, others small but yellow. What were they supposed to be looking for? Could be for their husband, the moon, who was coming from far, though the signs of his appearance were not yet clear.

Anaro and Lilly went straight to the verandah where the other girls were. The dance had not yet started. The organiser was still busy, arranging boys according to where they came from. They sat at the end of the courtyard. A table containing a record player, records, a kerosene lamp and a matchbox stood in the middle of the courtyard. One chair was placed near the table for the person playing the records. There were also logs of wood near the table for the *okembe players*. The dance was going to be mixed. Emou, Okwapa's father's house stood almost at the back of the latter's house. It had no lights, which meant that the occupants had gone to bed.

The organiser clapped his hands and everybody kept quiet. He was responsible for law and order and it was his duty to say who should dance because there were many boys from different villages.

It was also the duty of the organiser to discipline those girls who left their homes with the intention of coming to dance, but refused to do when asked for reasons best known to themselves.

"You are all welcome," Okwapa began. "I am glad to let all of you know that Mr Okiru, standing here, is the organiser tonight. Listen to him and if you have a problem, let him know about it. I am very glad again to inform you that our brother, Mr Joseph Ewiu is also here with us tonight. I think all of you know that he is a policeman, so please those of you who have been taking *waragi* and have come purposely to make trouble, are informed that the law itself is with us tonight. And I want to inform my sisters that you have come to dance, so I don't want to hear anyone saying she does not want to dance. I am also pleased to inform you that today we have the *Kakere Okembe* group.

On hearing about *Kakere Okembe,* boys cheered and whistled and girls talked together excitedly, pulling their *sukas* (sheets) around themselves more securely. Every girl covered herself with *esuka* when not dancing in order to keep warm. It could be cold, especially those rainy days. *Okembe* music was liked, if not preferred to record player music by almost everybody.

"So," Okwapa continued, "we will dance to *Okembe* music and record player music alternately. Now, which music should we open this dance with?"

"Okembe!" the majority shouted but there were a few who wanted record player music. "Okay," Okwapa said. "Where are the boys? Kakere boys, come forward and give us a tune."

The boys came out of Okwapa's house where they had been drinking local beer with Ewiu. They were five. They came out in a single file, each one carrying his musical instrument. These instruments were all the same in shape, the difference being in their sizes.

The first boy to come out had the largest *Okembe* and came out carrying it on his head. He went straight to the table in the centre of the courtyard. He put his instrument down and sat on it. He plucked the wires and it gave a deep rumble. Everybody cheered. The second, third and fourth boys came holding theirs in their hands. They ranged between medium to small size. The fifth boy carried two tins containing very hard seeds. The tins had a few holes on one side only, to let in the seeds or small stones. When he joined the others, he shook the tins, which he held one in each hand and the sound they made was sugar to the ears of the expectant crowd.

They sat on three-legged small stools in a semi-circle facing the boys, withtheir backs to the girls and the house. The boy with the largest instrument sat in the middle with the others on either side of him. Each boy had his instrument down in front of him, between the legs. They were all in khaki shorts and short-sleeved shirts like the rest of the boys. The boy with the largest instrument was also the biggest in the group and he was their band leader. The youngest was the one with the tins and also the soloist.

33

"Which tune should we start with?" their band leader asked them.

"Let us start with Aconyo, " the soloist replied.

"We are now ready," the group leader announced.

"Okay," the organiser said. "Since this is the opening dance, boys, where are you? Everyone get a girl. Start!" he concluded and rushed to the verandah to get himself a girl too. They danced in a line, each one facing his partner at the beginning but they kept on turning round and until they were facing the partners again - repeatedly; so that they danced face to face; back to back and side by side. The soloist sang.

Soloist	-	In Aconyo
Chorus	-	In Imaia Acamo Nambeya
Soloist	-	In Aconyo
Chorus	-	In Imaia Acomo Nambeya
Soloist	-	Otuno kotyeho
Chorus	-	Pige Wanga Keto Loi Loi
Soloist	-	Idyer Iwor Do
Chorus	-	Gunya Keto Dupe Dup
Soloist	-	Abuto Keto Tur, Tur, Pi Paro Abore In
Imia		
		Acamo Nambeya
Soloist	-	Ha! Ha! Ha! Kakere
Chorus	-	Oyee - ee -!!

After this, the music became instrumental only. All the band boys were dancing, with their heads twisting on their necks here and there, according to the rhythm of the tune. The song, accompanied by the *okembe* music, was repeated three times. Everybody was dancing vigorously, sweating. Dust, which could be seen in places where the dim light of the kerosene lamp fell, rose in the air. In other places it could be felt, breathed in, so that the irritation it caused made a few cough. Everyone liked this particular song and tune.

It was a sorrowful love song. When the soloist said, "In Aconyo", the boys with girlfriends substituted their names mentally instead of "In Aconyo" so that it became "In Angwaro", "In Aryekot", "In Atayo", or whatever the girl's name happened to be. Ewiu was so comfortable with a pot of beer, he didn't know that his would be "In Anaro". They were all dancing silently, apart from a few who were

34

both dancing and talking at the same time. They danced for about twenty minutes, then the players stopped. There was cheering, whistling and shouts for 'ncore'. Girls were not escorted back to where they sat. They were abandoned as soon as the players stopped. Boys also went back to their seats, sweat glistening on their faces. Everyone felt hot. If you didn't sweat, it meant you hadn't enjoyed the dance.

"Those boys can sure beat the thing," a boy said as he went back to his seat.

"Have you attended that of the Ocero boys? Those boys are also fantastic. Once you have heard them play, you will never attend a record player dance again."

"In fact I came because I heard the dance would be mixed," another said. "I prefer *okembo* dance; one feels more free."

The players went back inside where a fresh pot of beer was put before them. The dances usually were free but the *okembe* players played better when given beer to warm their insides from time to time.

"That was a fantastic tune, you sure can play," Ewiu congratulated the players.

"Thank you," the band leader said. "But I didn't see you dancing."

"I am going to dance," Ewiu said, "I was still busy with this beer. We seldom get proper home brew out there." They drank together as they talked. Outside, small boys were playing but big ones were busy looking for their "Aconyos". A boy would come to the verandah and call his sister or any other girl he was used to and ask her who the girl in a blue twist dress, or red dress was?"

"She is called Atayo or Iteo," the sister would reply.

"Go and tell her that I want her," the brother would say. "If the answer is yes, then let me find you with her under that tree, behind Okwapa's father's house."

"Okay," the sister would reply and proceed to arrange the meeting between the boy and the girl by saying to the latter, "Do you know somebody has sent me to you?" The girl would understand immediately and ask, "Who?" Then the sister would supply details by describing the brother's looks or type of clothes he happened to be wearing.

"Tell him that he will get his answer on Wednesday at Lwala

Market." But if the answer was 'No', the girl would simply say, "Tell him that I don't want." The sister then would try to plead on behalf of her brother saying, "He is a good boy and is a P.7 student in Lwala". If the girl meant 'No', she would then say, "Okay, he is an angel and in Lwala P.7, why don't you marry him, after all what don't you have?"

With those biting words, she would march back to the verandah, leaving somebody's sister hurt and not knowing how to tell the brother that the girl had rejected him.

The organiser presently came out of the house. The air outside was cool to his face but his stomach was warm because he had been sucking beer (kong ting). He clapped his hands and voices dropped to murmurs. "Now we are going to dance to the tune of the record-player. When it is *Okembe* dance, we will dance together but if it is the record-player, I will call one village at a time. Understood?"

"Yeah!" the boys answered.

"Okay now, Ochuloi boys will dance the next record please. Get your girls ready." Ochuloi boys ran to the verandah. There was nothing like, 'May I have a step with you please?' or simple bow. No. The boys just grabbed anyone who passed for a girl. Those boys did the choosing: the girls had no choice. The most important thing was for a boy to find himself a girl before the record started playing. A new Lingala record was played. It sang "*Kasongo yee, yee, mobali nangai...*" Rumba was the dance style at the time.

After sometime, boys released their partners and did what they wanted to do with themselves. They jumped up and down, wriggled, hopped or just stamped their feet. All was done facing the partner and to the rhythm of the music. Many danced so vigorously that despite the cold, they found themselves sweating. When the record came to an end, girls were abandoned and everybody went back to their seats.

"Lilly, escort me behind the house to pass water," Anaro asked her friend. While there, they heard the organiser say, "Will everyone get ready for the *Okembe*."

"But we have hardly rested," Anaro complained.

"Let us not go back to the verandah; we will hide here until it is over," Lilly said.

Ewiu felt like going for a short call too and went behind the house where everyone went for that purpose. As he was going, he noticedthat the sky was clear and bright in the east. The moon must be about to appear, he thought. He shivered as he felt the cold seep through his long-sleeved white shirt. He felt warm inside and a bit light-headed. The beer was starting to work on him. He turned a corner, and then came upon the two girls suddenly and stared at them speechless. The girls acted immediately. They started running away from him, thinking he was the organiser. He hurried after them, calling out, "I am not the organiser." They stopped and he asked them what they were doing there but they kept quiet. "If you don't tell me, I will report you to the organiser," he threatened and the girls felt frightened. They knew what organisers did to girls who refused to dance. Lilly spoke first, defensively. "My friend here is not feeling well. We felt that if we missed that record, the next one would find her a bit better. We didn't mean to hide."

"What is your name?"

"I am Lilly Aryeko."

"What about you?" he asked the girl who had not yet spoken.

"I am Anna Anaro."

"Are you not Okanya's daughter?"

"I am."

"Come with me, both of you," he said and led them inside. They found a mat and sat on it, away from the pot of beer.

"Don't you people drink? Come near the pot and drink. I am going out but don't worry, I am not going to report you to the organiser," he said and left. As soon as he left, the girls grabbed a straw each and sucked for about three minutes without a pause. "My," Anaro said disconnecting her mouth from the tube, "if it had been the organiser, we would have been in trouble!"

"He wouldn't have killed us, anyway," Lilly answered, feeling better and warm. They drank for about ten more minutes before Ewiu came back, followed by Okwapa and the *Okembe* players. It seemed Ewiu had briefed his friend about the girls because when he came in, he just smiled in welcome and greeted them. He sat down, called his sister and ordered for hot water which was brought and poured in the beer. Okwapa's house was a single room. It had a big forked piece of wood in the middle, supporting the grass-thatched roof. There was a bed in a corner with a table near it. On the table was a wooden box, some books and a kerosene lamp.

The boys sat on chairs around a medium sized pot of beer; the three girls on a mat between the organiser and the leader of the *okembe* group, facing Ewiu, Okwapa and other boys. They drank in silence for sometime, then Okwapa said, "What has tied your tongues, girls? Is it my visitor here?" he said, looking at Ewiu with a smile. The girls murmured shyly as they moved restlessly on the mat. "Or is it me?" Okwapa continued. "You all know that I am William Okwapa; this man here, is Joseph Ewiu, these are the players we are always meeting at dances. Now, who is new here?"

"Nobody," the girls said, looking down. Lilly was more uncomfortable. Okapa had sent a girl to her two weeks back, but she had not yet given an answer.

"Is that so?" Ewiu asked. "Does this daughter of Okanya remember me at all? I remember I left her a small girl but now...! Do you remember me, Anaro?"

"Yes, I do," she said, raising her eyes to his face. Then, suddenly, something happened to her. Her heart missed a beat or were they beats? She lowered her eyes, thinking that what she had seen was not bad.

She already knew that he was tall. Now she saw that he had on a long sleeved white shirt, black pair of trousers and blue canvas shoes. The hair was black, thick and curly, with a parting at the right side of the head. He had no beard. He was dark but not as dark as Okwapa.

"Yeah," Okwapa said, "do you hear that? I told you these small girls never forget people."

"Good thing they don't," Ewiu said, feeling light-hearted. He felt like dancing. "What about that tune again? *Aconyo*?" he asked the *Okembe* group band leader.

"Now?" the leader asked.

"Yes, now," Ewiu said. The leader left with his group. They started to play. "Willy," Ewiu continued, "my joints have rusted and I want these girls to help me straighten them."

"How can a joint rust!" Anaro and Lilly laughed.

38

"Come and find out for yourself," Ewiu said, getting up. He left the house with Anaro, followed by Lilly and Okwapa. They joined the line of dancers outside and fell in step with them. Anaro noticed that there was nothing rusty about Ewiu's joints. He knew how to dance, when to turn East, West, South or North. They danced until the players stopped. Then sweating, they went inside.

Lilly and Okwapa were already there. "Talking of rusty joints," Okwapa laughed, "who retired first?"

"Never you mind; I feel hot," Ewui said as he unbuttoned his shirt. He felt better. More beer was brought. They drank and danced all *okembe* tunes and changed partners. During the change of partners, Ewiu asked Lilly to tell Anaro that he wanted her. Anaro promised to give the reply the following day, after prayers. The dance closed at 3.00 a.m.

"We are going home," Anaro announced, getting her *suka* ready to leave.

"Who is staying?" Ewiu asked. Anaro kept quiet but she got up. "We are all going together. Let us wait for Willy and say 'bye' before we leave, not so Lilly?"

"It is okay," Lilly answered but she was also on her feet, her *suka* wrapped round her. Ewiu was watching Anaro. He liked her. She was in a blue twist dress. It fitted her well. She was the colour of an ant-hill, with long lovely legs. He wished he could see her face but she kept it averted from him. Okwapa presently came in. "Let us go," he said and everybody got out. Okwapa locked his door and then he led the way. The girls walked behind him and Ewiu took the rear. They walked like that, in silence until they joined the main road. "Willy?" Ewiu called. "I don't know about you but I am freezing!"

"Sure," Okwapa said, turning to face the girls. "What about covering us also?" The girls pretended not to like this idea. They were trying to by-pass Okwapa when Ewiu grabbed Anaro's sheet. Okwapa did the same with Lilly's.

"Give me my sheet," Anaro said, running after Ewiu, who was dodging her among the shadows. The moon was shining brightly. Lovely shadows of trees were scattered on the road. The silvery light of the moon lay on everything around. Ewiu kept on dodging Anaro until she became tired and warm. She gave up the chase and started walking towards the others. When Ewiu realised that she was not going to follow him, he turned back and enveloped her in the sheet with him. "See?" he said. "All I wanted was for us to share the sheet." He tickled her in the side and she laughed and edged away but he drew her back. They walked slowly, side by side with his arm around her.

"Did Lilly give you my message?" he asked in a lowered tone.

"Yes," she replied, feeling breathless.

"What about the reply?"

"Tomorrow, didn't Lilly tell you that? Won't you go for prayers?" she asked.

"Sure I will. Then tomorrow. How is your father?" Ewiu asked, changing the subject.

"He is all right." They could not see Lilly and Okwapa. They were the only people on the road. He escorted her until their big house was in view.

"I am stopping here," he said, getting out of the sheet and wrapping it around her properly. They stood facing each other, saying nothing for about three minutes. "Okay, see you tomorrow," he said at last, touching her left cheek gently, playfully, before he left. Anaro walked silently and quickly towards her hut, the feel of his hand still on her cheek.

Chapter Seven

Lilly sat in church, thinking about the events of last night which made her feel guilty. She turned to Anaro but Anaro was dozing off. She nudged her in the arm and whispered, "Wake up. The priest is looking at you." Anaro woke up with a start. She found the priest staring at her and as a result, other people near her were also looking at her. She pulled herself together and looked in front of her. Her head ached a little and she felt empty and nauseous inside. The priest concluded his sermon and prayers continued.

Anaro felt better and wide awake after the singing started. Someone behind her was making a lot of noise with the soles of his shoes. People turned to see who it was. Anaro also looked and her heart almost jumped out of her mouth. It was Ewiu, the man she had danced with at Okwapa's home. He was dressed in a white, long-sleeved shirt, a black pair of trousers and 'knocking' black shoes. Lilly looked at Anaro and smiled. Anaro looked down. She did not want to meet Ewiu's eyes when he came back from receiving Holy Communion. She remembered the promise she had made to him to reply to his question today, but what would she say? The answer of course was 'yes' but how would she bring herself to say the word? She decided she would keep quiet. After all, boys always say that when a girl says 'no', she means 'yes' and when she keeps silent, it also means 'yes'. Ewiu was going to be her first boyfriend. Others before him had applied but had been rejected. Holy Communion over, they prayed for sometime and then the priest said, "May God almighty bless you: the Father, the

Son and the Holy Spirit." Everyone got up and made the sign of the cross then answered, "Amen". This Sunday the sermon was about the good shepherd, and so the last hymn they sang was:

(1) *The Lord is my shepherded, there is nothing I shall want.*
   Fresh and green are the pastures, where he gives me
   respose.
   Near restful waters he leads me, to revive my drooping
   spirit.
(2) *To the Father and Son give glory, give glory to the spirit*
   To God who is, who was,   and who will be for ever
   and ever.

After that, everyone went outside, talked and greeted each other. School children went in two lines with their teachers behind them. Everyone went home but a great number passed through the hospital to see the patients, others went to buy Holy pictures from the priest or the nuns.

"Let us go and greet them," Lilly said.

"Who?" Anaro had not seen the people Lilly meant.

"Your sweet," Lilly said with laughter in her eyes.

"You mean those two?" Anaro asked. "I can see yours is there also." They were looking at Ewiu and Okwapa who were talking to some other boys. Okwapa was holding a bicycle. "Let's go to the hospital," Anaro suggested.

"Are we not going to greet them?"

"No. If they want to greet us, let them come here. In any case, they will also be going to the hospital." So they went, following the road which passed between the convent and the nurses' dormitory and continued to the hospital. On Lwala road junction, there was a big sign post saying **Lwala St Mary's Girls' School and Lwala Hospital.**

They went through the maternity ward. The entrance had yellow and red flowers, planted in tins and arranged on both sides of the door. The compound was neat, the grass looking green and well- kept. Here and there were flowerbeds. A big mango tree, directly in front of the ward, provided a good shade. Mothers and their attendants sat under

42

it while nurses made beds.

Anaro and her friend admired the nurses, especially their light blue uniforms, white collars and smart caps on their heads, which made them almost look like the nuns.

They left the hospital. The school was on their left as they went west. They could only see the big long classrooms, with white-washed walls. The statute of Our Lady stood at the entrance of the school, facing the road with flowers planted all around it.

"Did you enjoy yesterday's dance?" Lilly asked.

"Yes I did, very much," Anaro answered.

"Now, my dear, I was almost forgetting, what is the reply?"

"What do you think I can say?"

"Yes, of course."

"But who is going to tell him?"

"You don't know these town boys. Town boys are good," Lilly persuaded. "They can dress you smartly if you get married to them."

"Of course, if he marries you, but do you think he can marry a simple girl like me?"

"Why not?"

"My dear, those people want working girls."

"But not all of them," Lilly defended. "Look at Odella, he is also a policeman but he married a village girl."

"But that girl was from Senior Two. She only failed to get work."

"No, Anna my dear, this boy I know is good. He will not let you down."

Anaro feared to say 'Yes' for many reasons and yet at the same time she admired Ewiu and wanted him. They were walking very slowly. When they came back to the junction with the notice board saying **Lwala St Mary's Girls' School** and **Lwala Hospital**, they looked behind and saw Okwapa on a bicycle with Ewiu on the carrier.

"They are coming, Lilly, what shall I do?" Anaro felt excited, nervous and shy. "What will I say? Tell me quickly, what should I answer?"

"Say anything," Lilly said.

"I will say 'yes', Lilly," said Anaro before the two boys reached them and stopped. When Anaro greeted Ewiu, he retained her hand in his and said,"How are you?" looking into her eyes.

"I am all right," Anaro said and tried to pull out her hand but Ewiu held on.

"How did you find the *okembo* dance of yesterday?" he asked her.

"It was good."

"Do you always attend these *okembo* dances?" he added, with a touch of jealousy.

"Yes, but only those which are held not very far from home," Anaro answered looking down.

"How is everyone at home? They didn't come to pray today?"

Ewiu knew Anaro's parents. He was the son of Lakeri, the old woman Abeso had gone to consult. He had seen Anaro when she was a very young girl. Now she was a big girl. "They came for the first mass," Anaro said and pulled away her hand. She started pulling at some grass and putting little bits of it in her mouth.

"What is there at home?"

"Nothing," Anaro said.

"I am coming there this afternoon." Anaro kept quiet.

"May I come?"

"You can come," she said.

"I am not joking, I mean it," Ewiu said and looked at his friend who was trying to get hold of Lilly's handkerchief. "Let us go," he said loudly. Anaro liked his deep voice. Lilly came and pulled Anaro to the other side of he road, leaving the boys on one side.

"How are you getting on?" Okwapa asked his friend in a low voice. They were both walking, with Okwapa just rolling the bicycle.

"She is all right."

"Has Lilly given you the reply?"

"Not yet but I think everything is alright. Lilly is a good girl. Good thing she and Anaro are friends."

"I am going to Anaro's home this afternoon. Will you escort me?"

"Ha! ha! ha! man you are bold," Okapa laughed.

"No, all I want is to see her father. I am not going as her visitor. We are neighbours and friends."

"I wish you good luck. The man might become suspicious."

"No, I don't think so. Can't a man greet a neighbour just because a

44

neighbour has a beautiful daughter?"

"Well, maybe not but try to be careful or your girl will suffer. I remember last year I organised a fantastic *okembe* dance and Anaro came. A week after the dance, somebody told Okanya that Anaro was at that dance! Man, how the man beat that girl and her mother!"

"You mean he does not allow her to go to dances?"

"He does not approve of such things."

"How did she come yesterday then?"

"She just escaped when he was asleep."

"Imagine that! Anyway, I am not taking a long time there. Are you not coming with me?"

"I would come but there is something else I am going to do."

"I will come and tell you about it afterwards."

"Okay," Okwapa said. A blue Datsun pick-up passed, spraying them with clouds of dust. They ran to the bush to wait until it settled.

After they reached the junction, Anaro separated from the rest and took the path on the right, which led to her home. As she left them, Ewiu said to her, "I will be coming."

Chapter Eight

"Ha! Some people can pray; look at the sun. It is already one o'clock. Where have you been?" Abeso was displeased with because Anaro had taken a long time to come home after mass.

"You see, mother," Anaro said, "Father Rolland took a long time preaching about the 'Good Shepherd'. And then I passed through the hospital and I was kept talking to that nurse, Rose," Anaro lied. She had not talked to any nurse at all.

"How is she?" Abeso asked. Abeso had fallen sick sometime back and been admitted at Lwala Hospital when Nurse Rose had been on duty. The two had become friends. Thereafter she would send her daughters with things like oranges, eggs or milk to take to her. So the girls also got to know her. Now when Anaro mentioned Nurse Rose, she believed her.

"Where is everybody?" Anaro asked.

"Your father is inside, giving Ikiso tests in what do you call it - arithmetic," she said with difficulty and laughed at herself. She went to the kitchen carrying dry firewood. Anaro followed.

"What are you cooking, mother?" Anaro asked and looked into the pot. She saw dry fish already mixed with groundnuts. "Ha! we are going to enjoy ourselves. How did you get it, mother?" Abeso was busy pushing more firewood into the fire. She was boiling water for making millet bread. Anaro went and changed. She put on the blue twist dress she had worn for the dance the previous day; instead of her dirty nylon daily wear. Ewiu had said he would come to visit.

46

"Have you forgotten that your father went to the cattle market yesterday?"

"Father can be a darling at times. Let me go and thank him for my sandals again."

"Why are you putting on a nice dress? Where are you going?"

"Nowhere, but don't you know that today is Sunday?"

"Girls! Bring me plates from the *tandalo*, we are late with lunch already."

"I will be back in a minute," Anaro said, putting the plates down and going to greet her father.

"How was the service?" he asked as Anaro entered the house.

"It was okay but that priest, Father Rolland, took a long time preaching and then I passed through the hospital to see Nurse Rose."

"You mean that friend of your mother?"

"Yes, father."

"I see."

"Father, thanks a lot for my slippers. I did not thank you properly this morning because you were in a hurry for the first mass."

"Do they fit you well?" Okanya smiled, well pleased with his daughter.

"Yes, father, they fit exactly."

"Stand up, let me see." The slippers fitted her well. She was becoming a big girl. I wouldn't be surprised if I got a letter from Anaro one of these days, Okanya thought.

"Ikiso, where did you pass?" Anaro asked.

"I used the main road, but I ran all the way because I wanted father to help me with this maths."

"Ikiso is doing well but she is lazy. She can't think by herself yet when I ask her, she answers correctly," Okanya said.

"Really, Anaro; these things are difficult," Ikiso complained.

"Has she finished?" Anaro asked their father.

"She has almost finished. She is remaining with only four numbers," he replied.

"Lunch is ready. Ikiso, give me the small table, you will finish after lunch."

"But father will go way and who will help me?" Ikiso was tearful.

"I will do them for you," Anaro offered.

47

"I don't think I am going anywhere today; yesterday I drank too much," their father said.

"At the cattle market?" Anaro asked.

"No, it was at Esemu's home, it was very tough, the brew."

"It must have been for Ameso, their daughter. She is in my class, she told me about it," Ikiso said.

"Is she clever ?" Okanya asked.

"She is not clever and not a dumb, she is just in the middle," Ikiso answered.

"I am coming back with food, let me find the table clear," Anaro said and left. Ikiso removed her books from the table and put them on a chair in a corner. She left the table in front of her father. Okanya was passing his eyes through a geography text book. Ikiso also went to the kitchen.

"Ikiso, take the mat," Abeso said when she saw her. "And you, Anaro," she continued, "take your father's food. I will bring ours." Abeso left last, closing the door behind her. Only Okanya ate at a table. Abeso sat down on the mat with her daughters. She sat with her legs crossed and stretched before her. Behind her, her daughters sat with their legs folded under their buttocks, with their left hands touching the ground for support.

"Someone get me more salt," Okanya said.

"You eat too much salt" Abeso complained. "Ikiso, go and bring your father salt."

"Please bring my pepper as well," Okanya shouted after Ikiso.

"Where is my pepper?" he asked when Ikiso handed him salt in a calabash.

"Did you ask for it? I didn't hear: let me bring it." Ikiso went back to the kitchen and came back with a small branch of pepper tree. It was dry but the red peppers stayed stuck and could drop out only when shaken. Ikiso carried it with care and far from her nose, as it caused much sneezing when inhaled. They ate in silence for sometime.

"Who ate my eye?" Ikiso asked.

"I ate one, but one is here," Anaro said, giving Ikiso the remaining eye of the fish. Anaro and Ikiso always ate the eyes of the fish first, be it dry or fresh fish. The eye of a fish is oily and sweeter than the rest of the body.

"Ikiso, if I were you, I would eat the brain," their father said.

"Why?" both girls asked.

"The brain of the fish makes people clever."

"I don't believe in that thing." Abeso said.

"It is true," Okanya said. "Look at the Bakenyi who live along Lake Kyoga, they are very clever!"

"What happened to Musana, son of Kirya? He is a Mukenyi but has he not failed to pass Primary Seven?" Abeso argued.

"Maybe not, but most of them are said to be clever," Okanya said and drank water.

"Have you heard? You better work hard on the brain of fish," Anaro said and smiled at her sister. For answer, Ikiso put out her tongue at her.

"You have started. Why do you start misbehaving when you are satisfied?" Abeso said, looking at Ikiso with a reproachful eye. Ikiso looked down and said nothing. To change the subject, Abeso said, "You must have been very lucky yesterday to sell all the groundnuts."

"Yes, it was a lucky day for me yesterday. You see, when I got out to wash my face, the first person I saw was a man. I knew the day would be all right."

"Did your friend Orace also go?"

"Yes, but that man is a fool. He embarrassed me so much I had to hit him to bring him in line."

"Oh! What did he do? How did he embarrass you?"

"I will not drink with him again. Imagine after drinking beer of that good woman, Agenesi, the wife of Esemu, he refused to pay. I got mad and I hit him."

"I imagine you had a fight."

"No, we didn't fight. He felt ashamed and gave Agenesi ten shillings, after I had paid on his behalf."

"Now, why was he refusing to pay?"

"He was claiming he had a fifty shilling note only. He knew that Agenesi could not change that money. When I offered to change the money, he became rough with his words and I hit him, once only."

"Sorry, he must have said something very hurting."

"Indeed, it was so hurting the way he told me that I can't produce a son." Abeso felt sorry for asking. She said nothing more. It hurt her too much not to be able to produce a son. When a couple failed to produce at all, it was always blamed on the woman. She knew in her heart that people were blaming her. A man could never be blamed. Was it not from the body of a woman that the baby came? The people from Okanya's clan didn't know that some men could be sterile, and that it was a man who decided the sex of the baby. They knew that a child belonged to his father, because the father paid dowry for his mother.

Lunch over, the girls took the plates away for washing. Abeso went into the bedroom to rest and to think what to do about her pressing problem. She must go to Nurse Rose and ask for medicine to swallow; could be those European medicines could help her, she thought. Tomorrow I must go, she decided. Okanya was also brooding over the same problem. What will I do, he asked himself. Who will look after these girls when I am gone? He was still asking himself these questions when a bicycle bell rang. Who might that be, he wondered. He went out to see the visitor.

"Oh, it is you, Joseph! You are most welcome!" Okanya got the bicycle from Ewiu. "Go right in," he invited the visitor, rolling the bicycle to the shade. When he came back, Ewiu was already seated on a chair facing the doorway. He got up and they shook hands. "Welcome, son. Tell me about Kampala," Okanya said, sitting down.

"Kampala is all right, except that there is too much rain at present."

"When did you come?"

"Yesterday. I used *Saa Mbaya* bus and arrived here at 3.00 p.m.!" Okanya shook his head in wonder. "Where is the mother of Anaro?" Ewiu asked.

"She is in the bedroom resting. Let me call her." Okanya went to the bedroom. "Assistant, assistant, wake up. We have a visitor," Okanya said as he shook his wife gently.

"Who is the visitor?" she asked in a sleepy voice.

"The son of Lakeri?"

"Oh! When did he come?"

50

"If you mean when he came here, it is ten minutes ago. Now, here is money. Go and get some beer for him." Okanya handed his wife a ten shilling note and he went back to join Ewiu in the sitting room. "Ah, we are still as you left us except that they have brought us a new way of planting cotton," Okanya said, sitting opposite Ewiu.

"How is that?"

"These days we clear a large area of land together and after that, each person is given a strip for planting cotton only. No other crop is allowed. It is called 'Group Farming'."

"It sounds all right."

"It is okay except that it is a bit far. Imagine people from Ochyloi having to go to Lwala."

"Is that where it is?"

"Yes. This year it will be at Lwala, last year it was at Akum."

"Akum is near. Now, what happens to the garden when all the cotton is picked?"

"It is good of you to come to see us old ones." Abeso interrupted their conversation. She sat down, her dress full of creases. The blanket she had been lying on printed itself on her left cheek. Her eyes were red and she looked sick.

"I am also glad to find you still in good health," Ewiu replied politely.

"Oh, my son, don't be deceived; you are lucky not to find me buried. I was very sick, I was even given a bed in the hospital." All the time she was talking, she never looked at the visitor. She was busy rubbing her arms and scratching herself.

"I am sorry to hear that."

"It is true, she was very sick," Okanya said.

"What did the *Bikira* say the disease was?" Ewui asked her. *Bikira* was the local term for a nun. Our lady too was called Maria.

"The *Bikira* said it was pneumonia."

"Were you coughing very much?" Ewui asked.

"Yes, I was coughing and at the same time it didn't want me to breathe. Once I took in a deep breath or coughed, something like a needle would go through my chest and run to my back."

"Are you better now?" Ewiu asked.

"Yes, I am all right now. I got many injections. Daniel tried to apply

51

native medicine through incisions on my chest but it would not improve until I got those European medicines."

"Things have changed, Joseph, our native medicines can no longer treat some diseases, or are these new diseases?"

"No, I don't think they are new," Okanya added.

"But why do some not respond to our medicines?"

"Could be the people who knew the right medicines, people like your grandfather, went without showing all the medicines to your father," Awiu said.

"Could be, but my father showed me all kinds of medicines. I know the medicine for cough, for treating diarrhoea, measles and pains in the ears and many others," Okanya said. "Anyway, I think hospitals are the ones killing native medicines. Imagine only a headache can take someone to the hospital these days and yet when we were young, if you complained of a headache, your father would cut both sides of the temples and let blood run freely until it stopped by itself. I tell you, you would feel instant relief after that treatment," Okanya concluded.

"And the worst new disease these days is the false teeth, mostly attacking small children," Abeso said.

"Which one is the that? I don't know it," Ewiu said.

"Oh, my son, don't say you don't know it because you will know it soon enough when you marry and get a child." Abeso felt sorry for Ewiu.

"That one, Joseph, is a very funny disease," Okanya said. "Can you imagine a baby of two weeks having teeth?"

"That is why it is called false teeth," Abeso said. "They are not actual teeth and it can make the child weak, unable to suck, passing very watery diarrhoea and if they are not removed quickly, the child dies."

"It is really terrible. But who removes them?" Ewiu asked.

"Normally women are the ones who remove them, especially Acholi or Langi women. The disease is not new to them. It started there. It is just descending on us," Okanya said. Abeso got up and went out. She found Anaro helping Ikiso with maths. "You don't greet visitors?" she asked generally.

"We didn't know, mother, who is he?" Anaro asked. Anaro of course

52

knew who the visitor was, she had even seen him coming before she entered the kitchen.

"The son of Lakeri," Abeso said. "Your father has given me money to go and buy him beer, and I want to go with one of you to carry the beer."

"Let me go with you, mother," Ikiso said.

"You can't manage; beer is not water, remember. It is very heavy."

"I will manage," Ikiso insisted.

"Okay. Ikiso, let us go. Get that pot under the granary and get some cloth for carrying it," Abeso said and then added, "And Anaro, meanwhile boil water and prepare the tubes and wash that small pot, that one under the *tandalo*. Ikiso, hurry up; is the pot lost?" she called and Ikiso came back with the required pot and they set off for the home of Esemu where the beer was.

Anaro put water on the fire, washed the pot, prepared the tubes and went to greet the visitor. "You are welcome, visitor," she said as she entered the house. She knelt down and then offered her hand to the visitor. They shook hands.

"You have grown big, Anaro, what have you been eating?" Ewiu asked her. He was full of smiles, looking down at the girl who was also looking down. For a girl to look down when talking to a senior person was a sign of good manners and respect. You can look briefly but it is bad manners to stare.

"That one grows like a banana," Okanya said.

"She was in school, I remember."

"Yes, but I failed to get her school fees. She was accepted in Sacred Heart in Gulu for Senior One, but those people wanted 800/= plus many things which I was supposed to buy for her and where could a poor man like me get that from?" Okanya talked with much sorrow which wiped away smiles from Ewiu's face and made Anaro almost cry.

"What a pity!" Ewiu sympathised.

"My dear, what to do?" Okanya said in the same tone. "Anyway, don't mind much. She knows how to write and read, that is enough. Her sister, Ikiso is the only one in school now. I don't know if I will manage to push her further."

53

"Where is she?" Ewiu asked.

"She went with mother at Esemu's," Anaro answered.

"I remember I saw you in church today but I never saw her," Ewui said as though it was his first time to talk to Anaro that day.

"Can you pick her out when she is with other girls? The uniform makes it difficult to identify anybody," Okanya said.

"It is true, what you say because I was there today yet I never saw her. What are you cooking for the visitor?" Ewiu's teased Anaro.

"Food."

"What food?"

"You will see when I bring it," Anaro said and left the house. In the kitchen water had started to boil. Anaro busied herself with tiding the kitchen. Soon their mother returned, followed by Ikiso carrying the pot of beer. Ikiso was sweating and breathing hard. The pot was heavy.

"Ha!" Anaro said when she saw Ikiso. "Didn't I tell you? Now you are breathing like a goat."

Abeso helped Ikiso to put the pot down. "Bring the small pot I told you to wash," she told Anaro. She measured enough beer into the small pot and kept the rest of it. Anaro looked for an old tin plate and stood the small pot of beer on it, then she carried it to the visitor.

"So this is the food you have been cooking for me?" Ewiu said. "Thank you very much." Ewiu had known all along that something was being prepared for him. The whispered conversation Okanya had with his wife in the bedroom, and the disappearence of the lady made him know that he was going to be entertained, and what was more entertaining than the local brew? *Kong Ting,* the Iteso call *Ajono.* The Langi call it, *Kong Lango,* the Acholi , *Lacoi* and in towns it is known as *Marua.* Hot water and tubes were brought. Okanya sucked a mouthful and spat on the floor, then he made the sign of the cross, sucked and swallowed. It was better than when he had drank it yesterday. He handed the tube to Ewiu who did exactly as Okanya had done. Then he sucked several mouthfuls before handing the tube back to Okanya.

"The brew is very good, unlike what we get there," Ewiu said, looking up at the grass thatched roof. "Anyway I can't expect those women there to know how to do it properly. It is not only the Bantu

54

women trying to brew this beer, Iteso and Langi women also brew, but the taste is never like a home brew."

"Have you forgotten the old saying, 'Home is home'?" Okanya reminded him.

"Indeed it is true."

"Have you tasted their beer also, I mean the native brew of the Bantu?" Okanya asked, relaxing in his chair and enjoying their discussion.

"Yes, I did but never liked it. Moreover, it is drank like European beer, in a cup or a glass, and cold!"

"I heard that the men are the ones who brew, is it true?"

"It could be true but I have never seen it being brewed," Ewiu replied.

"I see," Okanya said. "Is it the one they call *Mwenge Ebigrere?*"

"Yes, but who told you about it? You seem to know a lot more about these people's beer than me."

"I once had a friend called Mukasa, who used to tell me about these things," Okanya said.

"Thank you very much, mother of Anaro," Ewiu said. Abeso had entered, carrying a tube and a mat.

"It is nothing, not enough to make you drunk," Abeso said. She sat down on the mat and started sucking with the tube she had brought.

"She says this is not enough, yet I feel I am getting drunk already," Ewiu told Okanya as though Okanya was absent when Abeso was talking.

"A drunkard, my dear child, will never say he is drunk,'" Okanya said. "If we had a big pot of beer, sure enough we would see you drunk, and that would be the time for you to deny having tasted any beer." They all laughed. It is always like that with beer. Once you start feeling hot inside, all your miserable burdens evaporate with the sweat and you start getting tipsy after the second water. Laughter comes easily and you are irritated easily but never worried. You can unburden your heart to strangers and become either rude, quiet or very talkative. Most people become talkative, that is why they say that 'Alcohol opens the mouth of a coward', Okanya thought. They drank and talked.

Third water was brought with more beer. "Anaro, do you want me to sleep here today?" Ewiu joked. He really meant to say 'thank you'. Beer always brought many words to the mouth.

"With only this?" Anaro said. It was proper the way she said it. The host would never accept or believe he had done enough.

"E-r, Joseph, I am very glad you came to see me today. The one who leaves his home to go and visit another is a good person and a friend," Okanya said. He was starting to get drunk. When Okanya was drunk he could never come to the point very quickly and most of the time he repeated what he had said many times before. Abeso was aware of all these signs.

"As I said," Okanya repeated, "the one who visits is a friend. Now, as a friend, I am going to ask you a question."

"Daniery, this child didn't come here to be questioned by you. Let him drink," Abeso said.

"No, let him ask me," Ewiu protested.

"When a man, and most of all, your husband is talking, you should keep quiet." Okanya looked at his wife with eyes which seemed to say "Don't interfere or else..."

Abeso got the message and said, "Okay, ask only one."

"Who said they were twenty?" Okanya said. Then he turned to Ewiu and said, "What I wanted to ask you is whether you haven't yet come across a Muntu girl there? Look at your mother now, she needs someone to talk to."

"I think—" Abeso started to say.

"Don't think anything," Okanya interrupted her.

"What is wrong with you today? What have you drunk, urine?" Abeso retorted. Ewiu wanted to laugh but he thought better not to. Anaro saw Ewiu preparing to say something and she went out. She stood on the verandah. She wanted to hear what he would say.

"Anyway, Mr Okanya," Ewiu said, "what you asked is good. I am going to answer you frankly that I am looking for a wife to go back with."

"That is the spirit," Okanya applauded and gave Ewiu his hand to shake. They were now laughing. Abeso just grinned at both of them. "I feared you might bring us a Muntu who can't brew beer."

56

"No, I can't make that mistake."

"Yeah! It is good to have a wife, though they can be very annoying at times," Okanya said and looked at Abeso.

"I am very grateful for what you have done for me and before I go," he said, getting a twenty shilling note which he gave to Abeso. "Please accept what drove me out of home." He gave Okanya also twenty shillings.

"Thank you very much," Abeso said.

"Thank you," Okanya also said. "Such is the one I am proud to welcome home."

"Anaro! Anaro!" Abeso called. Anaro, who was standing on the verandah, ran to the kitchen from where she shouted, "Coming."

"Come here," Abeso called. When Anaro came, she asked, "Is all the beer finished?"

"There is still some little left."

"Bring it here, the visitor wants to go."

When Anaro brought the beer, Ewiu said, "Oh, I forgot my hostess, here, use this for buying thread for plaiting your hair." He was admiring Anaro openly. Okanya had gone out to pass urine. Abeso saw his eyes and concentrated on sucking the beer.

His eyes were bright and dreamy. He felt hot. He had gone for a dance yesterday but he had not seen a girl who was as beautiful and as well dressed as Anaro.

"Thank you very much," Anaro said.

"It is nothing." He was eating her with his eyes. The way he looked at her made her also feel hot and uncomfortable. When Okanya came back, Abeso also went out. "You also drink," Ewiu said, handing Anaro a tube. She sucked while kneeling. "Sit down and drink properly." Ewiu just wanted to look at her.

"It was good of you to drop on us like this," Okanya said. "But it is a great pity you had to depend on bought beer. I always say that if food is bought, it is never enough!"

"It may be true," Ewiu said. "But I know that little food is sweeter."

"I hope you will come again," Okanya said.

"Sure I will," Ewiu said and got up. Yes, he was drunk but not very much. He felt dizzy for a moment but that was all. He got out and

57

Okanya followed. The day was coming to a close. The sun was just a yellow ball, far away in the west near the horizon. The sky was a clear blue sheet. No stars yet, save the only star the villagers called the 'husband of the moon'. The insects which feared the sun were starting to come out of their hiding places to sing praises to the departing sun, their god. Ewiu looked around him for the first time. Yes, Okanya had a clean compound; it was recently swept. The *Akulony* tree in front of Okanya's house made the place become dark quickly. Urine was killing him but not here, he decided. Okanya came back from behind the house rolling the bicycle.

"Where are these people?" he asked no one in particular. "Maria! The visitor is going," he called. To him alone was Abeso 'assistant'. When people were around, he called her 'Maria', and to the children she was 'your mother'. "Women with their kitchen," he said, shaking his head. He opened his mouth to say more but at that moment, Abeso came out of the kitchen, followed by her daughters.

"We are glad you came to see us," Abeso said.

"I am also thankful for what you did," Ewiu answered. Abeso reached the end of the courtyard and said, "We stop here. When a visitor is escorted too far, he does not return soon." She spoke on behalf of her daughters as well.

"Okay," Ewiu said and shook all their hands. When he saw Ikiso he said, "And where have you been hiding?"

"She just fell asleep when she was reading her books. She has just woken up," Anaro said.

"Oh! Ikiso, don't let those books put you to sleep, okay?"

"Yes, sir," Ikiso answered in a colourless voice.

"Greet Lakeri for us," Abeso called after the departing figures. Okanya escorted Ewiu up to the main road. There was no one using the road at that time. Darkness was eating hungrily the remaining light of the day. Boys hurried cows home, and big birds called their mates in deep tones. Everything on earth feared darkness, except the insects which sang brightly without fear.

"Have a good night and greet the old woman for me," Okanya said.

"The same to you," Ewiu said. "I have enjoyed the visit very much."

"We will see if what you say is true by your next visit." Okanya spoke on behalf of his family and himself. They shook hands and having nothing more to say, they parted. Okanya went home slowly. He was thinking of what Ewiu had said about wanting a wife to marry! Yes, he was now big enough but he envied the father of the girl Ewiu would marry! Ewiu had very fat cows, kept by his only uncle at Kakeno, not very far from Okanya's village.

Chapter Nine

Lwala stores had only one roundabout where roads met. Planted in the middle of the roundabout were sign posts indicating the directions of the three roads leading from it. There were three signposts, written on yellow pieces of tins arrowed at the ends. The letters were thick, black and plain. One signpost pointed south and read, **Kalaki 6 Miles**. One used this road when one wanted to go to Ochuloi, Kocila or Kolio. Another sign post pointed east and it read, **Otuboi 4 Miles.** The third one pointed west and it read, **Kaberamaido 11Miles.** Shops were lined on both sides of this road. A big market stood on the right, as one faced Kaberamaido.

Today was market day. It was a Wednesday. The sun shone brightly on the sweating bodies of men, girls and boys, selling and buying from each other. The market was a cleared area, not very big, with stalls for fresh and dry fish at the edge of the market near the road. Across the road from the market, there was a hotel called, **Nena Momot Hotel.** There was a big *kituba* tree behind the market. Many people who had finished to sell or buy things, waited for their friends under the large cool shade of this tree. Today Anaro was one of the many, sitting patiently; waiting for her friend Lilly. Anaro was sent to sell millet. She got only ten shillings because the millet was little. Her mother had instructed her that in case the millet got sold, she was to buy soap, salt, fresh fish and a razor blade. Money not being enough, Anaro had bought fish and salt only. She sat on the soft grass in her light blue 'twist' dress. Her glistening, oily hair was combed high on her head. Her bag, made from palm leaves, was in front of her and by the side of the bag lay her blue slippers. People passed before her eyes, but she did not know any of them. They were all walking with a purpose, it showed in the way they hurried along. They were dressed in bright coloured Nyanza textile materials. Most men were in khaki shorts and short sleeved shirts. Women were all mixed up. Married ones were in *gomases* and some in *sukas*. Girls were more fashionable in their different styles. The place was buzzing and bustling with activity. The market had mostly foodstuffs and things like soap, salt, needles, razor blades, and the like.

"I have been looking for you like a needle," Okwapa said, shaking hands with Anaro. He was in a black bell-bottomed pair of trousers. His shirt was open from the neck down to the breast bone, revealing a flat, black wide chest. Okwapa was tall, black and smooth-skinned. He was just starting to grow a beard. He had brown eyes with bushy eyebrows.

"Yes, I' m here," Anaro said as she got up and put on her slippers. "Why are you looking for me?"

"I have been sent by the one you know," Okwapa said. He rolled up his shirt sleeves. "He sent me to tell you to report to **Nena Momot Hotel** as soon as possible."

"I am still waiting for Lilly."

"All right, if Lilly comes then you come," Okwapa said and went towards the hotel. People stared at him as he went along. There were few boys who could be as smart those days.

It was almost noon and the sun was beginning to get very hot. What is Lilly doing, Anaro wondered. She wanted to go and see Ewiu very much. They had known each other for two months now and she was used to him and she liked him very much. It felt good to be with him. But why in a hotel? "Could be he wants to buy me something to eat," she said to herself.

Lilly soon came, her face shiny and oily. She had also combed her hair, which had much oil in it. They always used 'Nazi Oil'. It had a bad smell but it was believed to make the hair grow long and black and soft. Lilly was wearing a round-necked and sleeveless sack dress with white and red dots. She was fat, short, and black as night but

61

with a smooth complexion, white even teeth and wide round eyes. She came hurrying towards Anaro, holding a bag similar to Anaro's of *sansa*. "E—E—uh!" she said and dropped down near Anaro. "I am so hot, let me rest a bit before we go."

"They want us to report to **Nena Momot Hotel** as soon as possible. I have been waiting for you."

"My, what is it they want from such a hotel?"

"Don't you want a chicken?"

"But to eat there when home is so near! Anyway, we will go and see. Who told you about it?"

"Who else but Willy," Anaro said with laughter in her eyes.

"Oh! My Willy, what has he put on?"

"He is so smartly dressed, that if we don't hurry we will find him taken."

"I will hang myself if he is taken," Lilly said with a look of sweet memory on her face. "Have you seen Joe?" she asked.

"Not yet," Anaro said. Those days Joseph Ewiu had become 'Joe' and William Okwapa 'Willy'. The girls talked about nothing when they were together except Joe and Willy. And the boys in turn talked about Anna and Lilly most of the time. They were all in the cosy pit of love!

"What have you bought?" Anaro asked.

"My dear, I bought some fish and soap only. My aunt gave me sorghum to sell. You know how only few people buy it. I was even lucky to get eight shillings."

"It looked much. You sold all for eight shillings only?"

"No, some remained. I didn't want to stay burning under the hot sun anymore."

"Let us go." Anaro stood up. "And we must tell those people we are in a hurry to go home. If we just sit and talk and talk, you know how time goes when we are with them."

"It is true, we must let them know that we can only stay for a short time," Lilly agreed. "This fish I am carrying is for lunch. My aunt says she is tired of beans and she told me to hurry home."

They dusted the grass from their dresses, straightened themselves, wiped their faces and left for **Nena Momot Hotel.**

The hotel was a square semi-permanent building with a roof made

62

of iron sheets. The walls were smeared with black soil from swamps called *eriti*. The door of the hotel was made from old tins joined together with nails. On the wall, on one side of the door was written in white thick letters **Nena Momot Hotel** and on the other side of the wall there was a drawing of the Uganda court of arms. A two-roomed house, divided in the middle with a wall which had a door parallel to the outside door and the back door. The inside walls were also smeared with *eriti*. The floor was cemented. There were two wooden tables and two wooden chairs for serving meals. There was no menu as in bigger hotels.

Okwapa and Ewiu sat opposite each other at the table which stood at each corner of the small room. Anaro and her friend went in. The place was quiet. They stood in the middle of the room and looked right and left. They saw the boys looking at them and trying not to laugh. "We thought there were no people," Lilly said, going towards her boy. Anaro also went to Ewiu.

"Sit here." Ewiu put his right arm behind Anaro so that she leaned on his chest. "How are you?" he asked.

"I am all right."

"What do you have at home?"

"Nothing."

"Are you serious?" Anaro kept quiet and he tickled her. She laughed and said, "Please don't."

"Why not?"

"I don't know," she said. He smelt of Rexona soap and she feared that the oil in her hair might soil his shirt, so she tried to sit forward but Ewiu pulled her back. Now that Anaro was so near, Ewiu felt good. She was the one he wanted to marry. He had called her here to give her the letter! "We are coming there on Sunday," Ewiu said. "What do you say?" Anaro couldn't believe her ears! She knew Ewiu was asking her to marry him. "I have nothing to say."

"Please say something."

"But really, what do you think I can say?" she said with dancing eyes, which she was not allowing Ewiu to see.

"Will you not be happy to see us?"

"Oh! Of course I will be happy to see you."

63

"But do you love me?"

"You know I do," she said in a lowered tone.

"How were the parents when you left?"

"Father had gone to plough the Group Garden and mother to weed cassava," she said and looked at the other people. Lilly's eyes said "Let us go."

"We want to go," she said.

"Why so early?"

"It is one o'clock. Look at the sun outside."

"I have a bicycle, I will drop you home," Ewiu said, getting a letter from his shirt pocket and handing it to her. "Give this to your father," he said. Then raising his voice he added, "Willy, I think we can go now."

They were all leaving the room when the owner of the hotel said, "Are you not eating anything from this beautiful hotel of mine?" He was used to lovers coming to his hotel just to sit.

"Keep your food for travellers," Ewiu said with a smile and they left. Okwapa gave a lift to Anaro and Ewiu to Lilly to confuse anybody who might suspect anything.

It was at around two o'clock when they left and the sun was very hot and the market was almost empty, save for the fish mongers who always left last. The road was lined by people going to their homes. Women carrying baskets on their heads with babies strapped to their backs. Girls dallied behind in order to snatch a chance to speak to their boyfriends. Every time they passed a path leading to the main road, they saw lovers playing. Anaro sat on the bicycle with only a part of her buttock. It was the way girls sat on bicycles then. Women, mostly old ones, sat flat with both buttocks.

It was about 2.30 p.m when the girls were dropped off to follow their different paths home. They all said goodbye to one another and the boys left immediately but Anaro detained Lilly. "What are you going to do after cooking?" she asked.

"I don't know yet. It depends on what my aunt will want me to do. What is it?"

"Can't you come at ours? I have something to tell you."

Lilly was excited. "What is it about?"

"I will tell you when you come. I can't tell you now, we are late. If you can't come today, you can come tomorrow."

"No, I will come. I will tell my aunt that I forgot my hankie with you. She is not a strict woman."

"Okay. I will be expecting you."

"Mm, my dear, the old woman will eat me today. I am having her lunch, bye," Lilly said and hurried in the opposite direction

"Bye," Anaro called after her friend. She walked slowly, trying to think which time would be convenient to hand the letter to her father. Anaro feared her father. It was her mother who was simple to talk to. She decided she would give the letter to her mother to give it to her father.

Yes, I will give it to mother, she decided. She removed it from the bag and put it inside her dress over her left breast. No longer worried with the burden of the letter, she walked home happily.

Chapter Ten

From the garden, Abeso went to the well and took sometime bathing but when she returned, Anaro was not yet back. She cooked and ate alone. Ikiso was in school and her husband had not yet come back from his garden of 'Group Farming'. She looked at the sun from time to time which seemed to be going fast towards the west. She was worried about her daughter. She knew that if her husband returned before her, he would beat them both, especially herself because every mistake made by those girls was blamed on her. He was there to supervise, guide and correct big mistakes which he often did with a stick. Small things concerning those girls were the responsibility of their mother.

Abeso had become suspicious of Ewiu since the time he visited them and gave them money. Money was as sweet as life and yet Ewui had given generously. Why, she asked herself. If he was the one wasting Anaro's time, he would regret it. Abeso was restless; she could not sit inside, so she brought a mat and sat under the *akulony* tree in front of their house. She had not been there for long when she saw Anaro coming slowly. She looked at the sun and decided it was three o'clock. Anaro came straight to her mother, knelt down and greeted her.

"Before I say anything, hurry up and change your dress before your father returns." Anaro obeyed but she was not happy because her mother was annoyed with her. She never liked to annoy her. The great news she carried combined with the look on her mother's face killed her appetite for the food her mother had cooked. She put on her daily dress, put the letter under the mattress and then went out to her mother. The angry worried expression on her face had gone. She was feeling great relief. "You worried me very much," she said before Anaro could sit down. "Where have you been?" Anaro remembered the letter and smiled and Abeso also smiled voluntarily. Anaro was looking down. Yes, those were the changes in Anaro these days; she could not look one straight in the face. She was quiet most of the time and at times she could be so happy and active. "You can laugh, but if you had found him in, you would not be laughing."

"I am sorry, mother, but really Lwala is so far."

"I know the place is a bit far but since morning?—and look at the sun now, what time do you think it is?"

Anaro had nothing to say.

"You sold millet for how much?"

"I got only ten shillings, so I bought fish and salt only. I was unable to buy the other things you said to buy."

"Oh, my millet!" Abeso moaned. "What type of calabash did you use for measuring?"

"I used what others were using."

"Oh my millet! The person who bought from you must be thanking his God now."

"Mother, I won't be sent again." Anaro was near tears.

"Don't worry but I have to tell you if you are cheated or not. Now my dear, what is wrong? You don't want me to speak of my millet?" Anaro was bursting with anger! After going all the way to Lwala on foot and coming back on foot and her mother was not even thankful! She kept quiet, looking away from her mother. Abeso knew when Anaro was angry. She tried to make her forget her anger. "Are you not eating?"

"No."

"Let me see the fish you bought." Anaro pushed the bag gently towards her mother. "You have bought very good fish. How much?"

"Seven shillings."

"Only?" Abeso wondered. "The one who sold it must have done so thinking you were a nurse or a teacher."

"Mm, mother, stop teasing me. Do I look like those smart nurses?"

'You were very smart in that dress you had on, believe me."

Her mother knew how to scatter her anger; she was not angry now, so she felt like telling her about the letter. "Mother."

"Yes?" Abeso answered and waited but Anaro continued to write in the sand; just drawing lines. It was difficult to break the news. "What is it, Anna?" her mother asked. Anaro felt happy because her mother had used her Christian name Anna, which she often did when she felt motherly love for her.

"It is a letter."

"Whose letter?"

"Someone gave it to me to give to father."

"Is that all?"

"But I fear to give it to him."

"Why?" Abeso asked. She started being suspicious. "Who gave you the letter?"

Anaro felt breathless, she was sure that heaven and hell would drop down when she mentioned the one who sent the letter. "Ewiu," she said but nothing happened. Only her heart beat harder.

Abeso kept quiet for sometime and then said, "My daughter, there is nothing to fear. If you want your friend, why fear?" Abeso was inwardly proud and happy for her daughter. "When did he say they would come?"

"He said next Sunday, not the coming one but the other one."

"I see," Abeso said. "Where is the letter?"

"It is inside."

"If you fear to give it to your father, bring it here. I will give it to him." Anaro felt better. She ran to get the letter and soon returned carrying it in her hand. "So this is the letter?" Abeso said and tried to look as though she was reading it. She turned it upside down, she didn't know how to read. She was busy examining the letter and didn't see Okanya coming. He threw the axe down and came towards them saying, "Get me a chair." Anaro went in the house to bring a chair and Okanya saw the letter in Abeso's hand. "Whose letter is it?" Okanya had taken a long time without seeing any letter. He had nobody to write to, and no one to write to him. He had received a letter once from Ikiso's headmistress, inviting them for a parents' day at the school but that was two years ago. Abeso handed him the letter without a word. Anaro brought the chair and disappeared in the kitchen. She did not even greet him. She did not want to be present when he read the letter. Okanya sat on the chair and studied the letter. It was addressed to: Mr. Danniery Okanya, Omua Village. At the bottom of the envelope was written, 'By kind hands'. The one who wrote had a good hand writing and it was a man's handwriting. He tore the envelope and read the letter and folded it.

"What did it say?" Abeso pretended to be curious.

"Didn't she tell you?"

"She did not tell me anything," she lied.

"Anyway, from now on, you are going to be busy," he said. Abeso waited patiently.

"We are having visitors on Sunday, not the coming one but the next. Ewiu wants our daughter," he said and their eyes met and there was great understanding without words. Abeso kept quiet. It was not the place to discuss important matters. They would discuss it more at night in bed. "Call her," Okanya told Abeso.

"Anaro!—Anna!" she called. Anaro took a minute to arrange a humble expression before she went out of the kitchen. She went towards her parents with downcast eyes and knelt down while she waited for her father to speak. But he took sometime as though he was studying her, which made her uncomfortable.

"Anaro," he called as though she was far.

"Father," Anaro answered in a small voice.

"I hope you understand the step you have taken." Anaro said nothing. "Do you?" he asked.

"Yes, father."

"I know Ewiu, I know when he was born which was six years before you came into being. Do you want him?" Anaro kept quiet. "Anaro, I want you to answer every question I ask, because I want you to go when you want. I know I have been strict and it is good. I did not want to leave you loose to get spoilt. What you have done is good; but I want to hear with my ears if you want the man who has chosen you. Do you want him?" he repeated.

"Yes." Anaro was annoyed. Would she have brought the letter if she did not want him?

"That is good. That is very good. That was all I wanted to hear." There was a pause before he added, "And if you go, don't ashame us there; respect his people and don't forget to be generous, especially with food!" Okanya said and laughed abruptly. Abeso smiled and Anaro laughed but not at the joke but at the way her father laughed. "Yes, don't laugh, look at Orace's daughter, she is back at home and rumours say that she used to hide food under the bed, that was why she was sent back to her father," he said.

"I am going to advise her on all that before she goes," Abeso said. Anaro felt better, in fact she felt happy that the interview was over. She had expected her father to ask many questions which would embarrass her. Things like where she met him which she had feared most.

"Get me some water for bathing," he said and then turned to his wife and said, "Of course you will not forget to inform the women of the clan and the earlier the better."

"Oh, how can I forget that," Abeso said. Okanya got up to go and take a bath behind the house. His legs were caked with dry mud. He was in khaki shorts and he looked very tall and straight and almost happy. I must be born lucky, he thought, to wish for something and get it. He had admired Ewiu's cows long ago and soon they would be his. With such healthy fat cows, he would be able to do what he had always wanted to do, which had seemed like a dream before. He had wanted to buy a pick-up and start business. Selling groundnuts would have done, but it would take many years. And now— .

"Bring your father food," Abeso said.

"It is still on the fire getting warm," Anaro replied

"Then bring the table while you wait." Anaro obeyed and soon food was ready.

She brought everything on the small table before her father came back from taking a bath. She felt hungry; the fear which was killing her appetite was no longer there; so she remained in the kitchen to eat.

"When did you mingle this?" Okanya asked. The millet bread was

70

warm but hard. There was little water at the margin of the plate around the bread.

"It was not long ago," Abeso said. "It is those plates which spoil food. If it was in a calabash you would not have seen that water, and it would be hot."

"Then revert to using a calabash," Okanya said with a mouthful of food.

"You like using a table, so how can a calabash sit on that table?" Abeso asked.

"Oh well—" Okanya stood up. He had eaten very little food but finished all the vegetable. "I am going to see Oyuru," he said.

"Will you tell them about the visitors?"

"No, that is your work. I am going to tell only my brother," he said and left, whistling. He was pleased with himself. Abeso went to the kitchen and found Anaro still eating.

"I am going to tell people about your visitors," she said.

"All right."

"There is very little water left. You will decide among yourselves who should prepare supper, and who should go to the well. I know Ikiso is coming back soon. Give her something to eat first before you tell her what to do," she warned with a smile. Anaro could overwork her sister, she knew, even sometimes not give her food before the required job was finished.

"Where are you going first?" Anaro asked.

"I will go to Agenesi first, she is a good friend of mine. After that I will go to that rumour monger, Orace's wife, and lastly to Awao, your uncle's wife. Your father has gone there.

"Mother, won't you tell Atalo, Lilly's aunt?"

"You see Anaro, this is going just to be an introduction, it needs few people. I will tell the whole clan, with all our relatives, when it is time to go to Ewiu's to see the cows." Anaro was quiet. She wanted the aunt of her friend to come. "Anyway, for your sake, I will tell Atalo," Abeso said and left. "I want to come back and find supper ready," she shouted from outside.

"Yes—s" Anaro shouted back.

71

Chapter Eleven

The sun was losing some of its severity. Birds flew from tree to tree, visiting friends. It was time for the hard working ones to go back to the garden. It was just a small walk. He was passing through the small strip of land which separated their compounds. It was bushy but grass never grew on the foot path which passed through it. Birds flew away and rats escaped at his approach. Awao, the wife of his brother, Oyuru sat in the compound under the orange tree eating soil. She was pregnant. "What good wind blows you this way today?" she asked as she got up to get him a chair.

"Do I need to be blown? I just came and I am here," Okanya said laughing.

"How are you?" she greeted him.

"I am all right."

"How about Abeso and the girls?"

"They are all doing well. Where are the children?"

"Epaju and Omino are in school." Those were her boys. She had five children. "The rest went to look for mushrooms," she added, putting a piece of soil in her mouth.

"You women amuse me, now what is that soil supposed to do to the child?"

"They say it makes the child strong," Awao said, tightening the sheet over her chest. She was a short, brown woman, with large round eyes which looked more beautiful during her pregnancy. She wore a *suka* tied around her waist and sat with her legs stretched in front of her.

"Where is my brother?" Okanya asked.

"He has gone to chase away birds from our millet garden. It is just starting to get ready, but I tell you, birds are finishing it."

"Why does he not tie a cloth on a stick and plant it in the middle of the garden?"

"I think he will have to do that or else we will not harvest anything."

"That is how I have managed those birds myself."

"Should I go and call him?" she asked.

"You are already tired, don't disturb yourself."

"Ha! ha!" she laughed. "Who said I am tired? I have been sitting here since after lunch."

"But you are tired, see how you breathe."

"Oh! please don't tease me," she said, rolling her large beautiful eyes.

"Which garden has he gone to?"

"He has gone to that garden of ours across the road near Atalo's home. The one with the *ogali* tree."

"I know the garden. I will just go there," he said and got up.

"Use the path behind the house. It is the shortest cut."

"The mother of Anaro will be coming to see you."

"What news does she bring?"

"News about Anaro."

"Does Anaro want us to drink 'hot water' (marriage beer)?

"I think so," Okanya said and disappeared behind the house.

***

After her parents had left, Anaro started to prepare supper. As for water, that would be Ikiso's business, Anaro thought. She wanted Lilly to find her free so that they could discuss things. She worked quickly and happily and soon the fish she had bought was on the fire. What next? Nuts! Yes, that was the next thing to do. She jumped into the granary, got a small calabashful of groundnuts and went to shell them in the kitchen. The place was so quiet, it made the shelling sound very loud. Anaro was thinking of so many things that she did not see Lilly

73

come until she was smiling at her in the door way Lilly was dressed in an old dress which looked like a maternity dress. For some obscure reason, the fashion was known as *kitooro*.

"Hi, my dear, are you preparing lunch or supper?" Lilly asked.

"Supper."

"So early—why?"

"You don't know how dark this kitchen can become after 6.00 p.m."

"Don't you have a kerosene lamp?"

"Yes, there is one but it stays in the big house."

Lilly sat on a mat near Anaro and started to help her. "Now tell me what it is you promised."

"Joe wants us to get married, my dear, can you believe it?" Anaro said with a smiling face. She stopped working.

"When?"

"Soon. They are coming for introduction next Sunday but one."

"I had guessed right."

"Could be Willy told you."

"No."

"And now I am so worried about what to wear that day."

"Your blue dress can do."

"And of course you will come to escort me to get the money."

"Oh! Anaro my dear, who will escort me to get mine when you are gone?" Lilly was starting to miss her friend.

"But there must be some other girls from Kadie who can escort you." Kadie was the village where Lilly came from. It lay some few miles east of Lwala.

"Yes, there are a few smart girls there," Lilly agreed.

"I don't know who would have escorted me if you were not here."

"What about Ikiso?"

"No, I would not want Ikiso to escort me. Maybe Ameso, daughter of Agenesi."

"Where is everyone?" Lilly asked.

"They went to scatter the good news." They looked at each other and laughed. "When will you and Willy decide?"

"Soon, I think. We have even talked about it. He told me to wait till people have harvested millet, so that there would be plenty of beer."

74

"I think Joe is in a hurry because his leave is ending soon. Anyway, the major celebrations will be after the harvest, could be in August or November."

"I told you Joe was serious."

"But do you think I believed you then? Now you must pray I don't come back with a missing front tooth."

Lilly laughed and then said, "You can really be funny. Do you think he can beat you so soon?"

"My dear, men of these days can even slap you on the first day he takes you to their home."

"Those are the uneducated ones."

"Oh, Lilly, forget education! The more they are educated, the madder they get. And do you know their trick?"

"No."

"They beat their wives at night behind locked doors."

"But I hope Ewiu will not be like that."

"I don't know, I only pray he does not beat me."

"But one day he will have to beat you."

"Oh, Lilly, don't say that. Suppose he beats me there in Kampala, how will I run back here?" Anaro was now worried because it could happen.

"Anyway, as he is a policeman, if he beats you, you report him to his officer in charge."

"Then where will I be when he comes back from getting the punishment?" Anaro shivered.

"Anyway, I know nothing will happen to you. Joe loves you very much."

"I am sure he does. But they always do in the beginning."

"My dear, let me tell you the maddest thing Willy told me."

"Yes?" Anaro answered expectantly.

"Willy wants to join the army."

"Sure?" Anaro expectantly.

"He said that as soon as we marry, he will leave me with his parents and then go."

"Let him join."

"I told him I didn't like the idea but he did not listen."

75

"And suppose he joins and then he is transferred where Joe is?"

"Oh! That would be nice." .

"Let us pray for that and let us pray he goes through," Anaro encouraged her friend. They finished to shell the groundnuts and Anaro started to fry them while they continued talking. Ikiso came back from school at 5.30 and greeted them and changed from her uniform into a *suka*.

"Eat and go and fetch water, mother said," Anaro told her.

"But I am so tired!" Ikiso complained, wrinkling her face.

"I know you think I am doing nothing."

"I didn't say that, but really you can also imagine coming from Lwala on foot and having to go to the well now!"

"What will you do when Anaro goes?" Lilly asked her.

"Mm, where is she going?" Ikiso asked.

"She is going," Lilly insisted.

"Don't tell her," Anaro begged.

"Lilly, come and we eat," Ikiso invited, her face more relaxed.

"How do you know I have not eaten?" Lilly said.

"I know you have just come," Ikiso said and settled on one corner of the mat and started to eat. Ikiso's presence made talking difficult, especially talking about Willy or Joe.

"I am going," Lilly announced..

"Am I the one sending you away?" Ikiso felt suspicious. "Not really, Ikiso. You see, I have been here since we came back from the market."

"That cannot be true. How could you go to the market in that dress?"

"I went home to change and I had lunch then came. Ask Anaro."

Ikiso looked at her sister but Anaro ignored her and turned to Lilly saying, "Wait for me to pound these groundnuts then I will escort you."

"No," Lilly protested. "That will take too long. I deceived my aunt that I was just coming to collect my handkerchief; and now see how long I have stayed. Don't worry about escorting me.

"No. I can't let you go unescorted," Anaro insisted and looked at her sister. "Ikiso, pound these for me then I will escort you to the well." Ikiso started to argue but when Anaro talked about going to the well with her, she said "Okay," and resumed her eating.

"I hope to find you ready when I come back," Anaro told her sister. "When the food on the fire is ready, you can put it down."

"Where has mother gone?" Ikiso asked but Anaro and her friend were already gone.

***

Abeso decided to visit Esemu's home first. Agenesi, Esemu's wife, was her friend. She would let her into the secret first. She was happy and she knew that it would not be good to appear happy when asking for help, even from a friend. So she decided to put on a worried expression so that when village women gathered at the well to collect water, instead of saying, 'The way Abeso is so proud that her daughter is marrying a policeman!' They would say, 'Ah! Those who are having important sons in-law are also in trouble. Abeso is so worried, especially about how to get tables, glasses and breakable plates.' Abeso smiled to herself. She had heard such talk many times. Anyway, she was not worried. Ewiu was not a European. He grew up in the village, not in the town. She knew that when people went to towns, they behaved like white people. Things like women eating at tables. were things of the towns only.

She joined the main road and faced north, towards Lwala. There was no one on the road. Only a boy in shorts crossed the road, bringing a herd of cattle before him with a stick in his hand. A small dog followed him. 'Cows,' Abeso thought, 'we will soon have ours if all goes well.'

They had no cows of their own; that was why they could not plough so many gardens. They could use money to help them dig and Okanya had joined Orace who had a plough and an oxen to pull it, but despite their friendship, Orace would want to plough all his gardens before giving Okanya a turn to use the plough. Okanya would feel hurt but could do nothing.

Abeso walked leisurely. The sun was not hot but she knew that if she hurried she would sweat. Soon she turned left to a path leading straight to the home of Esemu. Agenesi was under their tree which was in front of the kitchen. She was sorting out beans from millet. Her daughter sat near her doing the same. "Anaro's mother," Ameso whispered to her mother.

77

Agenesi looked up and her face broke into a smile. "Who is that looking like the mother of Anaro?" Agenesi said.

"She is the very one," Abeso answered.

"You are welcome," Agenesi said, then turned to her daughter and said, "Get that hide skin for Abeso to sit on." It was a hide of a cow, cured and clean. "Why bother. Where is a good dress needing a hide?" Abeso quipped, smiling as she looked down at her not very new dress.

"My dear, soap matters, even if the dress is old. Wherever you sit, the price of soap has gone 'over the hill' anyway."

"Thank you, my daughter," Abeso said as Ameso handed her a lovely cow's hide to sit on. It was all brown, with irregular patches of white here and there.

Ameso knelt down and greeted Abeso before continuing with her work while the two women talked together. "What is that you are doing?"Abeso asked as though she could not see what Agenesi was doing.

"I sent the wife of Orace to buy me some beans for planting and this is what she brought me."

"Where did the millet come from?"

"I had sent her with some millet to sell. She sold some and the remainder she mixed with the beans. Anyway, I am about to finish sorting it out." She paused and then she said, "You didn't go to the market today?"

"No, I remained behind to try to weed. My dear, I will be the last to eat millet this year."

"I thought your garden, the one near the swamp, is about to get ready."

"Oh! Only that one, do you think I will manage?"

"Why not?" Agenesi asked ignorantly.

"Birds are finishing it and with this new problem which has dropped on me, I don't know if it will do." Agenesi knew that Abeso was about to say something, so she straightened up and looked at her.

"What is it?" Agenesi asked. "Is your husband deciding to do the funeral rights of his father?" Agenesi knew that since Okanya's father died a year ago, the funeral rights had not been done. It was an expensive ceremony which some people did after many years. And most people cemented the grave during that time.

"No, it is not about the funeral, it is about my daughter, Anaro," Abeso told Agenesi. Agenesi looked up with great surprise. 'Anaro who is guarded like a prisoner' she thought and smiled.

"When will they come?"

"Next Sunday but one."

"Mm, and who is our in-law going to be?"

"The son of Lakeri."

"Really!" Agenesi said. "He looks a good boy." Ameso looked up. She was getting interested in the discussion but she did not say a word.

"Oh! That is how they look in the beginning but as time goes on, they change."

"Sure, but some keep up the spirit."

"Yes but few." Abeso paused and then said, "And that is what brought me here today. I ask you kindly to bring me food when coming to greet the visitors. I can't expect more than food since the whole thing is so abrupt."

"Is he not going back soon?"

"I don't know but I think he has stayed for a long time... Where is my husband today?"

"Your husband has been gone since morning, I don't know where he is. He could be getting drunk somewhere."

"I must get going," Abeso said and got up.

"Are you not waiting for food?" Agenesi invited.

"That is for you. I will eat some other day. I have to hurry to tell others also."

"How many families have you visited so far?"

"Yours is the first. Please remember to tell my husband what I said," Abeso said as she was leaving. Agenesi escorted her for a short distance.

"I am stopping here," she said. They had reached the end of the courtyard. "When a visitor is escorted too far, she does not return," she added, shaking hands with Abeso.

"Oh! I am not a visitor, this is my home," Abeso said. "Greet my husband for me."

"Okay. Greet my husband also and my children," Agenesi said. It was their way of talking to call a neighbour's husband 'My husband' and her children 'My children'. Abeso left in better spirits. Agenesi was easy to talk to. She would never say what she thought of one in one's presence. She was a wise woman. She knew when to praise and when to sympathise. Abeso went from one home to another, telling them all about the coming visitors. It was dark by the time she went back home.

"Did you tell everybody?" Okanya asked.

"I did, except the wife of Orace. I can tell her tomorrow when we meet at the well."

"No, you can't tell her at the well, you know what things they can say later."

"In that case, I will have to go there after coming back from the garden tomorrow."

"Now, what are you going to do?"

"About what?"

"Well, will the visitors not drink anything?"

"Oh that, I have my flour of *kongo* ready. I wanted to sell it and buy a dress, but now I will have to brew it for the visitors."

"That is good," Okanya said. He felt better. Buying beer for the visitors would be very expensive. They were in bed and the kerosene lamp had been put out. They shared even the blanket, but since Okanya started drinking Abeso had wanted to separate the beds, but Okanya would not hear of it. So she still had to put up with his snores at night and the quarrels after she punched his nose to silence them. But gradually, she got used to the snores as she had got used to cigarette smell and many other things.

She could sleep these days even if Okanya's snores shook the house. She also became used to talking in darkness. They often discussed important matters at night, and since giving him what Lakeri advised her to give, Okanya had become good to her. He bought her things before she asked, and could even ask for her advice about a problem concerning them both.

"Did you find Esemu at home?" Abeso did not hear, she was deep in her own thoughts.

80

"Are you asleep?" Okanya asked.

"No."

"I said was Esemu at home when you went there?"

"No, why do you ask?"

"I was thinking of asking him to help me build a small shed for the visitors."

"What about Oyuru, can't he help you?"

"He can but I am not going to ask him. Things have never been all right between us since we quarrelled, you see." He paused and then said, "I know Esemu will help me if I ask him— even Orace."

There was sudden lightning followed by a noise like a big drum being beaten from far away. "It is going to rain," Okanya said almost to himself. Abeso was already fast asleep. It rained the whole night.

Chapter Twelve

It was almost dawn. Okanya got out of bed, wrapped in his blanket and got out of the house to check on the weather. It was very cold outside and the whole place looked miserable and too quiet. He went behind the house to pass water. He used his latrine for more important matters. A wind blew and lightning played tricks on the eastern side. It was a pity it was going to be a dull day because he had wanted to start preparations for his visitors.

"No work today," he talked half to himself, and half to his wife who he knew was awake.

"What are you saying?" Abeso asked, uncovering only her face.

Okanya went back to bed. "The weather is not good. A strong wind is blowing eastwards where large black clouds have gathered." There was lightning which lit their small room through cracks in the wall, followed by thunder, resembling the heavy running footsteps of an angry warrior. "Do you hear that?" Okanya whispered. The thunder was fierce. Abeso made the sign of the cross and said nothing. They could hear strong wind wrestling with trees, houses and other things. Trees wept, grass just whistled in wonder and sat down, but houses stood stubbornly unbending to the assault. There was another frightening streak of lightning followed by thunder, before it started to rain. Women rains, they called them because they were fat and they started one by one, pat, pat, and then in unison, fell in big heavy drops. Wind hissed and thunder growled in answer to the slashing lightning. It looked as though someone was using a big calabash to pour the water down. Okanya's grass-thatched house tried its best to keep water from going through but it failed. It first dropped on the wooden box which was not pushed far enough under the bed. Okanya ignored the warning, in fact he felt warm and was beginning to doze when he felt a large drop on his head. He thought that was the only drop so he moved his head away from the spot and tried to sleep but no, the drops became too many to be ignored.

"Get up," Okanya told his wife. "Let us move to the other corner." They did that but it was leaking there also. So in the end they folded their bedding together, and stood in the only dry corner in the room. They were both wrapped in their blankets standing close to each other, saying nothing. They could hear 'tok-tok' noise coming from the sitting room, a sign that it was leaking there too. The wind continued sweeping rain on the back wall from outside. Okanya knew, according to the direction of the wind, that if it continued that way, the wall would collapse! There was slashing lightning answered by thunder. It seemed as though lightning had told thunder that 'that is enough' and thunder seemed to have answered, 'please yourself' because rain stopped abruptly, leaving only a drizzle. This was called 'men rains' and it was the best because it could be absorbed by the soil easily.

Abeso looked annoyed! It showed on her face. Okanya wondered what was amiss. He wanted to know. "What is the matter?"

"Don't you know what is the matter? Look at all that water on the floor I worked so hard to beat and flatten!"

"Yes, but it can't be helped, it is nobody's fault."

"Ah!" Abeso grunted with anger. "With all the grass I cut for this house, if I really had a man who knew his job, that water would not be there."

"What are you trying to say?" Okanya was starting to get annoyed.

"Orace maybe a drunkard but his house never leaks," Abeso said tartly.

"Listen, woman," Okanya said, now very angry, "I spent days arranging grass on the roof of this house, if it is leaking it does not mean that I have done my work badly. You know how heavy today's rain was. On the other hand, if you feel that Orace is better than me, you can go to him," Okanya snapped at her which made Abeso more annoyed.

"When I talk of the house, you change the subject."

"No, I didn't," Okanya said. "When you praise Orace like that, it means you prefer him to me."

"I am not cutting grass for this house again."

"You are going to do it and you are doing it today as soon as the weather clears, so that I can repair those leaking spots today."

"I have too many things to do, you know that."

"You can tell Ikiso not to go to school so that together with her sister, they can help you to carry the grass home."

If I had power! Abeso thought to herself. Okanya stepped into the sitting room. It was a mess! The floor had patches of water here and there where it was low. Water was on his table, on plates used for covering pots and on one side of the wall, there was a long crack where water was running along down to the floor. Okanya felt like visiting the latrine, which was some yards away from the house. The matter was important and pressing but it was still drizzling outside. He got a winnowing tray which he used as an umbrella and left the house looking like a big mushroom.

"We are all going to cut grass for repairing our house. You will miss school today, Ikiso. It is too late and wet to go."

"It is all right, but what will I tell father?"

"He is the one who told me to tell you not to go to school," Abeso said. They had made a big fire in the kitchen and they sat around it on small logs of wood, warming themselves. Ikiso was happy she was not going to school. The dew on the short footpath from their home to the main road would be too much.

"Good morning everybody!" Okanya greeted as he entered the kitchen. He was in khaki shorts and a long-sleeved shirt. Drops of water winked from his tough curly black hair and his face was still wet from the washing. "Someone get me a chair," he said and shivered a bit. Anaro looked at her sister with eyes which said, 'You go'. Ikiso obeyed and brought the chair from the main house. "This house did not leak," Okanya said starting to enjoy the fire. "And yet some people were blaming me for bad work." He looked sideways at his wife.

84

Abeso was enjoying the fire too. The best way she was doing it was by turning sideways, away from the fire. "I did not blame you, but really you can remember, I am sure, the heaps of grass I cut for that house."

"Yes, I know you worked very hard, but surely the rain of last night and this morning was unusually heavy. I am sure some houses collapsed last night."

"Has it stopped drizzling?"

"It has. The sun will appear soon."

"Anaro, make some porridge for us. There is *cwaya* in a calabash in that pot behind you," Abeso said. *Cwaya* is a sour fruit soaked, squeezed and used for making porridge when there is no sugar. Too much of it causes diarrhoea, especially in children.

"Ikiso, get *cwaya* and soak it," Anaro said, making fire in another cooking place. They had three cooking places. Ikiso obeyed. Porridge was ready soon and Anaro served it in calabashes which she passed around. They ate it sitting where they were, around the fire. Okanya finished his first then he went to start his work. After cleaning the dishes and sweeping both houses, Abeso, with her daughters, each carrying a hoe, left for their work. Okanya, with the help of a wooden ladder, climbed on the roof of the house to see the bad spots. He found them easily. Ants called *edidi* had eaten the grass from several places. He removed all the eaten grass, now rotten and threw it down to be replaced by new grass which his children were supplying him with.

The weather was clearing. The sun smiled on the miserable shivering vegetation and soon they gave up being miserable and started being happy again. Wind passed and they all danced, getting rid of their burden of water. The evaporating air was humid and heavy. The few clouds which were left hanging about after the rain were all running away from the advancing sun, leaving a clear sky.

Okanya worked on. He was starting to sweat and his body itched a bit, especially his arms because of handling the new grass. His back felt tired too. He straightened up a bit and as he did, he saw Esemu coming towards him. Something was amiss. It showed in the way Esemu carried himself.

"Good morning, brother," Esemu shouted in a worried tone.

85

"What is the matter?" Okanya asked,

"I have come to borrow your ladder. We never slept at all last night! We stood the whole night."

"So did we. The rain was too much!"

"Ours was worse!" Esemu said shaking his head. "The kitchen collapsed. It broke all the pots."

"It didn't trap any child inside?" Okanya was worried.

"No, it was leaking so much that the children had no where to stand. So they came running to our house, which was also leaking everywhere, save in one corner. We gathered in that corner till morning."

"It was terrible! Anyway, I think it was for washing away the last pollen from the millet. Next month some people will harvest."

"I think so. Can I take the ladder now?"

"How will I come down. You wait a bit."

"Can't you jump down? You are still young," Esemu joked.

"Ha! ha! you want me to break my neck? Do you call a man whose daughter is getting married young?"

"Yes, she is your first daughter. If she were the last, I would agree with you."

"In fact I was coming there to ask you to help me build *goga* (a shed built with grass only, used for celebrations).

"Well, when do you want to build it?"

"Will next Friday be all right? They are coming on Sunday."

"It will be all right. Next Friday is still far."

"Okay. Thank you very much."

"Don't thank me. We all have daughters. And ten to one I will be calling on you for the same problem." Esemu felt better after voicing his problem to his friend.

"When do you intend to build another kitchen?" Okanya asked.

"Not soon. I think I will do it after harvest. I will ask my wife to brew beer so that I can call people to help me."

"Yeah! If you do that, it will be all right." They talked while Okanya worked. Anaro and her sister came carrying grass. They put their burdens down then greeted Esemu who was sitting on a chair, away from where Okanya was working. Ikiso threw one bundle of grass to her father but he had finished his work.

86

"Don't throw anymore, I have finished. Keep those for building the *goga*. You can tell your mother to come back, unless she wants to cut for the *goga* as well."

"Let me go and do mine also," Esemu said and left, carrying the ladder over one shoulder. He met Abeso coming back, carrying grass.

"Well done," Esemu greeted.

"How are you?" Abeso answered.

"I am all right, except that last night's rain made our kitchen collapse. It broke many pots."

"Oh! That was bad," Abeso said, her left hand on her chin, as a sign of sympathy.

"Ah, wife, we stood the whole night. The children, luckily, ran to our house before the kitchen collapsed."

"Indeed, that was providential," Abeso said. "Even us, we stood while it rained. The whole house leaked, but luckily for us, the kitchen did not leak. The children slept peacefully."

"It's the small ants which eat the grass, causing these leakages."

"It must be, because I had cut a lot of grass for that house of ours."

"It is so. Okanya has thrown all the eaten, rotten grass down. Ah! What shall we do to get rid of these ants? The day is still long, so I won't say goodbye."

"Okay," Abeso said and continued homewards. Her daughters had left her talking to Mr Esemu and were already at home.

Chapter Thirteen

"Oh, you are welcome," Rose said. "Come in here," she added and led Abeso to a room. "Please sit here while I go and tell my friend that I have a visitor." She closed the door and left.

The room where Abeso was taken was an examination room for pregnant women. It had one bed and a chair only. It was a small room with white washed walls. The top of the bed almost reached the only window in the room whose curtain was drawn back to let in light and fresh air. The wall opposite the bed had a nail on which a crucifix hang. Yes, that was how it was with all the wards and rooms of Lwala Missionary Hospital. It was easy to feel God's presence when one entered the so-called hospital which actually was a dispensary. Each ward was named after a saint. Abeso was in one of the rooms in the maternity ward which was named after our Lady, Mary the Mother of God. Her friend Nurse Rose was a nurse-midwife. The door opened and she came in and closed it.

"You are welcome," she repeated. "I hope you did not feel lonely."

"No," Abeso said. "I was busy admiring the cleanliness of the house."

"That is good," Rose said and went to sit on the bed. She was tall, black with thick black curly hair. Three quarters of her head was covered with a large white cap which covered the back of her neck, falling gently over her shoulders. She almost looked like a nun. She wore a light blue uniform with a round white collar and three white buttons on the front of the dress. She also wore brown laced shoes. She looked smart and the white cap on her head made her almost look holy. Now she sat with her hands humbly folded in her lap. The missionary-trained girls had good manners. After greeting her visitor, they talked about many things. Then Abeso said, "My monthly sickness disturbs me a lot."

"How?" Rose asked.

"You see," Abeso said, embarrassed, "I used to be sick when the new moon had just appeared, but these days I see it when the moon is young, when the moon is in the middle and when the moon starts coming out late at night."

"I see, but does it pain you when it comes?"

"Not much , only on the first day."

"Is it much?"

"Sometimes it is much, sometimes it isn't."

"But how old are you?"

"Actually I don't know how old I am, but I do know that I was born during the Kabaka's regime when there was so much hunger that parents sold children for a basketful of millet, or so my mother told me." Rose laughed. How could she know when that was. Some of the answers to such questions during antenatal clinics could be amusing. A woman could say she was born during the time when the sun married the moon (eclipse) and when swarms and swarms of locusts visited the world! But she could guess at a person's age just by looking at them. Abeso could be about thirty years old, she decided. She gathered that Abeso's monthly period was irregular and that might be the reason why Abeso was not being able to conceive. She was still a young woman. She decided to give Abeso some pills. She went out and came back with two packets of pills. "Now," she said, " I am giving you this medicine so that you may have your monthly sickness when the moon is young only."

"Oh, thank you very much."

"But you must take these tablets one by one," Rose said and instructed her fully about the pill. Abeso was very happy.

"And now, Rose, will you be able to come to my home next Sunday?"

"But I don't know where your home is."

"I will tell Ikiso to come for you."

"Will there be beer?"

"There will be a lot. Anaro is getting married."

"Really!" Rose said excitedly. "I will come."

"That is good," Abeso said. "But I am worried about one thing."

"What is it?"

"I don't have a good tablecloth for covering the table where the money will be displayed."

"I will lend you mine."

"Thank you very much. I think I can go now."

"Thank you for coming to see me."

"I am ashamed to have brought you only this," Abeso said, giving Rose a bag. Rose peeped into the bag and saw fresh maize.

"Maize!" she exclaimed. "Thanks a lot." Abeso never visited Rose without taking her something. She could even take her beer on big days. Rose was a Langi girl but she enjoyed the local beer very much. "Let me take it home, I know you need this bag for marketing," Rose said with a smile. She went to her home and was back soon with the bag in which she had put the table cloth Abeso had asked for. It was a metre and a half long, white, with flowers neatly embroidered into it with light green and blue thread. It also had lace around the edges and looked very beautiful. Rose escorted Abeso up to the main road, on the **Lwala Hospital** signpost.

It was around 9.00 a.m when Abeso had left home with the excuse of going to see Nurse Rose about the table cloth and to invite her to attend the occasion. She was not going to let anybody know about the pill. Every night she prayed God to give her just one more child, and how glad she would be if the child was a boy! Since Orace fought with her husband and mentioned that they had no son, it had never stopped paining her! She did not know what had gone wrong with her. Could be some woman with an evil eye had 'hidden her uterus'! But who? Okanya's mother would have been the first suspect but she was dead. She wanted a son very much. Who would look after her girls when they were dead? A brother was most important to a girl. When the girl married, her brother also got married because the dowry became

90

his to use. But now, Abeso thought, who was there to use our cows when they came? No, God should be more lenient to an orphan like me. Okanya's brother never liked us, Abeso's mind continued turning and worrying . She was so engrossed in her thoughts that she did not feel the hot sun. It was noon. She soon came to the footpath and branched off to her home.

The whole week was spent making preparations for the coming visitors. Okanya, with the help of Mr. Esemu built *goga*. Abeso worked together with Anaro. They threshed four big basketfuls of millet and when well mixed with cassava, it was taken to the flour mill at Lwala for milling. They went to the small forest behind Orace's home and collected firewood. They went there three times, each time coming back with big bundles which made them sweat and made their necks seem to grow shorter. While they worked together, Abeso instructed her daughter about men in general and what was expected of her when she got married.

"Do not ashame us when you are there," Abeso said. "You are marrying a big man and as a big man, he will have big visitors. Welcome them with a smile and always keep the house clean."

"I will try," Anaro answered.

"You must. It is no good running from your husband because of a silly quarrel. Let me tell you that when you come back home, no man will want you again. They will call you 'second hand.' Look at Orace's daughter."

"But they say that she was sent away because she was hiding food under the bed."

"Yes," Abeso said. "If she did. It could be exaggerated, I mean, how could she hide food under the bed? But all the same you must give them what they want."

"But I think he is taking me to Kampala, so I will have nobody to give food. The people who want food so much are here at home, and his mother is just alone. Where are his people?"

"His father's brother stays at Kakeno, three miles away from here. That is where they are. You will see them on Sunday."

"But, mother," Anaro sounded worried, "suppose he beats me one day? Where can I run to?"

91

"No, there is no where to run, and don't give him an excuse to beat you. If you see that he is annoyed or when he starts a quarrel, don't answer him, keep quiet. Answer him only when he talks to you. Men always want to feel important. If you show him respect, he will feel good and will not beat you, unless he is a woman beater by nature. But never try to run away from Kampala in case he beats you. Bear it all until you come back home."

"I hope he will not beat me. I fear a beating very much."

"No, my daughter, there is no need to fear," Abeso said and lowering her voice, she told her about the leaf Ewiu's very mother had given her. "I will divide it between us," she told her. "But you must make sure he does not see it."

"Oh, I will try to be careful."

"Another thing is, there are women there who will try to confuse you, telling you about Ewiu's old girlfriends. Don't listen to them. Since it is you Ewiu married, there is no need to worry. Jealousy without cause is no good."

"How do you know that, mother?"

"I know because women are the same everywhere. When I was brought here, women told me so many bad things about your father and his family; a certain woman even told me that Okanya's father was a wizard who killed people. But I never saw or heard of any person your grandfather had killed, may God rest his soul in peace! My mother had warned me of such people. I am now warning you."

"But I was taught in school that Kampala is a town of the Baganda and they speak Luganda. I don't know that language, how would the women talk to me, anyway?"

"No, my dear, a town has all types of tribes. You will be surprised to find that your nearest neighbour is a Kumam. The women who will come to you will not be Baganda. They will be Kumam, Iteso, Langi or Acholi women. Those you can communicate with without difficulty." Anaro wondered how her mother knew all these things when she had never been to Kampala.

Abeso continued to teach and warn her daughter as they worked. They borrowed plates, chairs, drums for cold water, large saucepans for cooking and boiling hot water for beer and two big tables. Okanya

92

went to the cattle-market at Otuboi and bought a big basketful of dry fish. They had groundnuts. The fish, with the goat he was going to slaughter would be enough. A chicken was never cooked for the in-laws before payment of the dowry was done.

Chapter Fourteen

The day broke like any other but in Okanya's home, it was an important day and more important to Anaro who was about to leave home. It was the long awaited Sunday. Anaro and her sister went for the first mass. Their parents did not go for prayers that day. They had to stay and organise the cooking and make other necessary preparations for the visitors. The girls came back soon after prayers and Ikiso went to the hospital for Nurse Rose. Lilly was already at Anaro's home, dressed in her red spotted dress. She wore blue slippers and her black face was oily. There was too much Nazi oil in her hair which she had combed high. A goat had been slaughtered and was on the fire in a big saucepan. At the other cooking place was another big saucepan with the dried fish and the third one was being used to boil water. All the cooking was done outside, in front of the kitchen.

"How are you feeling?" Lilly asked her friend. They were behind the kitchen, where Lilly was oiling and combing Anaro's hair.

"I feel bad."

"But why? I feel excited."

"It is because it is not you who is going."

"But I will go soon too."

"And I know you will not feel excited on that day."

"Anyway, I know it is the feeling of leaving home," Lilly said. "Imagine leaving home for good and coming back only as a visitor!"

"Oh, Lilly, it is terrible!" Anaro's spirits were down to zero. "I wouldn't worry if I were not going so far away. I know he is taking me to Kampala."

"Imagine to the city!" Lilly said, laughing. "Aren't you lucky?"

"I don't know."

"You will be having electricity in the house with an iron sheet roof. No more leaking grass house for you." They both laughed.

"Oh Lilly, you know how to make me stop worrying. We better go inside, the visitors will be here soon." Anaro was in her blue twist dress. It made her look more brown and beautiful. She also wore her blue slippers. She was taller than Lilly, with long lovely legs.

They went to the big house and sat on chairs. Sitting down on a mat would crease their dresses, a thing they didn't want.

"Look at this!" Lilly exclaimed as her eyes fell on the table cloth which was nicely spread on the table. "Where did you get it from?"

"Is it very nice?"

"It is killing!"

"Mother got it from Nurse Rose."

"It is so nice; if I were you I would copy its design."

"I am gong to copy it or ask Nurse Rose for her copy. What do you think I am going to be doing there if not making table clothes?"

"Surely, that is the only work town women do," Lilly said "Are you going today?"

"You know I am not going today. They will come for me another day."

Lilly heard voices and peeped to see if they were the visitors.

"Are they the ones?" Anaro asked, her heart jumping to her mouth.

"No," Lilly said. "It is Esemu, Orace and who is that one?" she asked, moving away a little from the window so that Anaro also could see.

"That is Nurse Rose and Ikiso. Are you blind?"

"Ah, yes, she is the one and isn't she smart! I can see women coming. I think they are carrying food."

"People will eat today and vomit. All that food!"

"Yes, that is what they want so that they can say, *Nywal beer*' (it is good to produce).

Ikiso came in with Nurse Rose and their mother came and greeted

95

her, obviously pleased to see her friend. She did not stay long. She went back outside to welcome women who were bringing food. After putting the food in the kitchen, they sat on the verandah of the kitchen and their husbands sat on the verandah of the big house, talking, joking and laughing, while waiting for the visitors. Okanya was busy preparing straw tubes, seeing to chairs and so forth. He looked smart in his long sleeved blue shirt and black pair of trousers. Some men were in trousers and others were in khaki shorts. Their shirts were of different colours, but the majority of them showed preference for white shirts whose whiteness some of them failed to maintain. Abeso was in a *gomas* with large red and blue roses on a green background. Most of the other women too wore *gomases* but there were a few who were in dresses and *suka* wraps. Almost all the women had head-ties. They all tried their best to conceal their excitement. They talked and laughed. Women continued coming, carrying food, only Oyuru's wife brought a pot of beer. Anaro was her daughter. Was not her husband from the very womb which created Okanya?

Every one was waiting. Anaro was becoming restless, her nerves were on trial. Lilly kept looking through the window from time to time.

"We are glad to welcome you to our home," they heard Okanya say. Lilly went to the window and peeped. Ah! Yes, there was Willy and Joe, both so smart! Joe was in a grey suit and Willy was in his black bell-bottomed pair of trousers and a blue T-shirt with 'Joseph' written over the breast pocket. Anaro's heart beat a bit loudly. Nurse Rose looked at her and not to let Nurse Rose get any ideas into her head, she joined Lilly at the window. Outside women were quiet but men were talking, laughing and greeting each other. All the visitors sat inside the *goga*. When everyone was seated, Okanya got up to welcome the visitors officially. "I welcome all of you to my home. I received your letter and I am glad that it is a neighbour who wants to be somebody more - a relative. When such a gesture is made, I know that I am good. Ebwonyu, am I not good?" Everybody laughed. Ebwonyu was Ewiu's uncle.

"Yes," Okanya continued, "it is said that a dog goes where it is given food. Now without any more delay, I would like the proceedings to begin. Oyuru, will you bring the table here please." With those words,

Okanya went and sat on the three legged stool behind the four members who were to negotiate the dowry. Each side had four members.

The table covered with the nice cloth was brought and put in front of the visitors. Ewiu's uncle removed a thick handkerchief and passed it to the man next to him to count the money. They had brought three hundred and twenty shillings. The man counted the money and returned it to Ebwonyu. Ebwonyu got up, cleared his throat and looked at everybody like a V.I.P inspecting a guard of honour and then he said, "Yes, it is true when it is said that a dog goes where it is given food. I know that Okanya is a good man, that is why when my son told me of his intentions, I told myself that, yes, why not? Okanya is not a wizard and nor was his father. His mother had never poisoned anybody's child. I knew my son had made a good choice, and I told him so. A beggar may know that when he goes to a certain place he will be given something, but when he reaches there what does he do? He begs. So my friend, we have come to beg for friendship, so that when anyone of you passes that way and asks for water, he or she will also be given food. Now, I put on this table the question mark, we want the answer. Those are my words," he said and sat down after putting money wrapped in a handkerchief on the table. He held himself in a manner which commanded respect. Ewiu sat near Okwapa, just behind Ebwonyu. They sat in silence. The whole compound was quiet, save for the women's side where mothers talked to crying children.

Anaro and Lilly were still standing at the window looking out when Oyuru came in. He was a funny man at times. Today he had tried to be smart. He called himself 'The minister of the poor'. "You have heard everything, now go, what are you waiting for?"

"Are the speeches finished?" Lilly asked.

"Yes. Now hurry up, I am hungry. Are you going out there looking like a sick goat?" The girls laughed. Yes, that was better. Anaro felt her stomach becoming cold. She had great fear of going out to get the money! Moreover, everyone would be looking at her! Even Lilly could not help being a bit nervous at this critical moment but she tried hard not to show her fear.

"Let us go now," Lilly said. "Don't look at anyone in particular.

Just look straight ahead at nothing." Lilly knew her friend's fear, but they had to go.

They walked slowly, side by side. Then on reaching the table, they knelt down and Anaro took the money from the table. Ewiu's uncle started to clap and everyone followed his example. The clapping did not stop until Anaro had handed the money to a member of her father's side, and gone back inside. Now that everything was over, Anaro felt better though beads of sweat still stood on her upper lip and on her nose.

Outside, negotiations began. First, the member who was given the money, counted it before giving it to Anaro's father. It would be divided between his wife and Anaro, each taking a hundred shillings. The remaining twenty shillings would be for the other family members. The first family member to speak was Esemu. He got up, cleared his throat and looked as though he would say nothing, then suddenly he started to talk, saliva falling from his mouth like simsim from a hot pan. He said, "The question you asked is now answered. That alone has already made us brothers, so I am going to talk like a brother. To seal the friendship more permanently, you know you will have to pay us something. We are not selling her, we have a lot to sell besides a person, but we want both of them to understand that they are marrying according to our customs. I know that all of you know that our daughter is very good and to console our loss we ask for only twenty cows, ten goats, and five hundred shillings - what do you say to that?"

"I have nothing to say to that," Ewiu's uncle said, getting up. "But as you know, we have children who need milk at home and she herself will need to be fed well. I can't agree to overturn my pot in one spot. For that matter, I beg you kindly to leave me five."

Esemu whispered to other members to agree to allow them pay fifteen cows only.

"That is fair," the second member said.

"No," member number three interrupted. "With all her education, they should pay at least eighteen."

"Be careful," number four said. "Remember things can go wrong and paying back all that can be difficult."

"Okanya is still a strong man. Moreover, the higher they pay, the better. The girl will fear to trouble her father and the man will have little hope of recovering his property if he sends her away. So they will always stick together," the third member insisted. They talked and argued but in the end, it was generally accepted on both sides that the dowry should be fifteen cows, six goats and three hundred shillings.

All these things were discussed between men only. Women sat and listened anxiously, waiting for the arguments to end so that they could eat and drink. Negotiations had to be settled first before proceeding to anything else. It was not until 3.00 p.m that they ate. After that there was a lot of drinking. Anaro stayed in the big house surrounded by envious young women trying to educate her about ways of men. How to behave and what to do to win a man. Anaro just laughed. Her mother had told her a lot and she would do as her mother told her.

They drank until 6.00 p.m. They then left, promising to come back after three weeks for their wife. Anaro saw little, if anything, of Joe that day, but when they were leaving, her mother came to tell her to go and say 'good bye' to the visitors. She was drunk but only moderately. She was all smiles when she came to Anaro, beer always made her like that. "Visitors are leaving," she announced from the door way.

"I should be going too. I am on duty tomorrow," Rose said.

"Come and escort these visitors, all of you. Follow me," Abeso said. She led the way. Anaro caught up with her mother. She wanted to know how everything had gone: the dowry and when she would leave. "Mother, how is everything?"

"Fine, my daughter. We are proud of you." She was smiling broadly. Beer can make people happy! Too much smiling made her face look tired and short.

"Say 'goodbye'," she instructed. "I will tell you more when you come back. Now hurry; we have a lot to do." She disappeared in the kitchen. Some distance away from the house, Anaro could see her father and some of the boys who were serving. They all looked cheerful and carefree. They were talking so loudly that anybody with good ears could hear them from two miles away.

Anaro and her friends caught up with them and they all became quiet abruptly.

99

"We will be glad to see you as you have said," Okanya said, shaking hands all round. Then he left together with the serving boys.

"My daughter, your father and mother are good people, a good tree bears good fruits." Anaro was kneeling down in front of Ewiu's uncle, looking down all the time as expected of a well brought up girl. "You will be a good girl," Anaro heard him say.

"Yes," she answered humbly.

"We are coming back for you after three weeks," he continued, raising three fingers in the air. Ewiu was restless. He knew that when his uncle was drunk, he could talk a lot, so he tried to let the old man understand that they wanted to go. He looked at Lilly and said, "Uncle, this girl too wants to say goodbye to you."

"Oh," his uncle said, shaking Lilly's hand. "Who is your father?"

"Yowana Ejabu."

"I know him, a man of courage. He killed a buffalo alone in a lonely part of the forest when we had gone hunting. We thought he had got lost, but soon discovered that he was chasing the animal - a great fellow." All the time he was talking, he was looking at Okwapa and Ewiu. He wanted them to know that the girl kneeling in front of him was the daughter of a great man in the days when they were still young. "How is he?" he asked

"He is all right."

"That is good. When you go back, tell him that I still remember him." Lilly was getting tired of kneeling down but there was nothing she could do. Nurse Rose, seeing that the talking was not coming to an end, entered the bush like one going to pass water and disappeared. She found her way back to the compound.

"Where are others?" Abeso asked her.

"They are still there. The old man's speech can't end and you know Lwala is far."

"It is true Lwala is far and it is getting dark. Look where the sun is, soon the chickens will go to sleep." Chickens went to sleep at 6.00 p.m, the last hour of sunshine, they believed. Abeso went inside the kitchen and got some cooked meat, covered it properly and put it in a basket. "Let us go," she said. "Lwala is far. I will escort you up to the junction." They went, using the bush path to by-pass Anaro's group.

The old man must have left because they could see only Anaro, Ewiu, Lilly and Okwapa.

"There is *okembe* dance at Lwala today, will you come?"

"I don't think I will be able to come today. You know that our clan people are still there. No, I can't come."

"Please do come," Ewiu begged. "Those people are all drunk now."

"It is difficult," Anaro said. Ewiu looked hurt, making Anaro's heart sink. So to save the situation, she had to promise him that she would try to escape. They said goodbye reluctantly. Ewiu's spirits were high, knowing that they would dance together that night but Anaro knew that with so many people around, it would be difficult to escape. She didn't make it that day. The women made ululations when Anaro joined them where they sat drinking beer. They were sitting in one half of the *goga*. Women sat down on the grass which covered the whole floor. They sat near the pot of beer in a circle. The men sat on chairs behind the women, also in a circle. Each man sat behind his woman. They had long straw tubes while men used short ones. Everyone was singing drunkenly in nasal tones. Some were completely asleep, especially the men.

"Our daughter, come here and we greet you!" one woman said.

"Yes, move near, let me touch you," another woman was saying.

"You have made us reach Kampala, the city," said yet another proudly, savering the thought .

It was getting dark, so after greeting the women, Anaro went to bring the kerosene lamp. After sometime, everybody left except Orace and Esemu. Okanya was already shaking his house with his snores, as was Ikiso. Only Abeso and Anaro were on their feet. Abeso was taking hot water for the remaining men when she heard them talking, sort of backbiting them. She checked herself and decided to listen to what they were saying. Who was there to see her eavesdropping? Every one was gone.

"This man must have something," she heard Orace say. She knew their voices, in fact there was nobody from their clan whose voice or footmark Abeso didn't know.

"How do you know?" Esemu asked, ignorant of what Orace was trying to say. Abeso did not understand what they were talking about.

101

She wanted them to mention the name of the man but they didn't. Instead they came to the point which made Abeso say 'so!' in her heart. "How can one say something and the other one just agrees. When you said twenty cows, I was happy with you. I knew that from such a high number it would then come to something like ten, eight or even seven. Things are no longer the same. My mother was married with thirty cows, but that was those days. We are in modern age now. Do you see my point?"

"Don't let such things worry you, brother."

"I am not worried that he will get fifteen cows. No. What I am trying to tell you is that this man seems to have powerful charms which make everything go the right way all the time. When we go with him to the market, his groundnuts usually get sold first before mine. What do you think can do that if not a charm?"

Esemu did not like the way Orace was talking. He knew that Orace was feeling bitter because his daughter was sent back to him before cows were brought, but whose fault was it? Certainly not Okanya's. Esemu touched Orace's knee in a gesture of friendliness. "My friend," he said, "walls have got ears, we will discuss that point some other time, okay?"

"I hope you will not sell me," Orace said.

"You can trust me," Esemu assured him. Then raising his voice, he called Abeso to bring them the last hot water. Abeso went back quietly to the kitchen, the water she was carrying was cold. So, she said to herself, it is true when they say that the one who eats from your hand is the killer! She remembered how she used to entertain Orace! Everytime they went to the market, he passed by to drink or eat before going to his home. All those pots of beer! All those chickens! She could not think of anything Orace had not eaten from their home. Welcoming him happily as a friend of her husband! To hell with friendhsip! But when she went back with hot water, she behaved in the most innocent manner and talked happily with them until they left. It was midnight when she joined her snoring husband.

***

The sky looked like a newly swept compound. Orace joined the main road and faced south towards Kalaki. He was not alone on the road, he met people and by-passed others. Some on bicycles, others on foot. When he approached a small hill, He came down and started rolling his bicycle along. I am getting old, Orace told himself. Long ago when he was a boy, he would stand up and ride until he had gone over the hill, then when he reached the top, he would sit and roll down without touching the brakes. But that was long ago. Now when he got to the top of the hill, he climbed on the bicycle again and he rolled down slowly, using the brakes.

He reached Kalaki as shops were being opened. He bought cigarettes, then left, using a path that branched off on his right. After riding for about five minutes, he disembarked as he approached a mango tree opposite Akeso's home. A boy got out of the house to receive him and after greeting him, took away the bicycle and stood it against a granary. Orace remained standing in the compound while the boy took the bicycle away.

"Come to the house," the boy told him.

"Is your mother in?"

"She is not my mother, she is my aunt."

"Is your aunt in?" Orace repeated.

"Yes, she is in."

Orace was feeling very nervous. He feared wiitch doctors but what could he do? He had to find the cause of his bad luck and Okanya's good luck. He entered the house and was given a chair. He sat down. This must be the sitting room, he thought. The door at the side maybe leads to the bedroom. The boy went through it and he could hear some murmured conversation. The house was grass-thatched, with mud walls. The floor was flattened and cow dung had recently been smeared over it. One corner had a mat and near it a pot of water stood on an old basin turned upside down. The pot was covered with a plate and on which there was a clean calabash. Above the water pot on the wall, there were two calabashes hanging from nails driven into the wall. The outside of the calabashes were decorated with black markings and dots. These were on Orace's right.

On his left there was nothing; the room looked bare. When he looked up the grass looked new. It is a new house, he decided. After about five minutes Akeso came out, sat on the mat and greeted him. Orace had never seen Akeso; he had heard of her from friends. He got the directions to her home also from friends who told him freely without asking. He looked at her and his earlier fear of witch doctors disappeared.

"How are the children?" he heard the woman asking.

"They are all right." He noticed her eyes - friendly and honest.

"The rain last night was so fierce. Where do you come from?"

"E—r. I come from Ochuloi," he stammered. He was busy observing the woman's skin - smooth and brown.

"Did it rain in Ochuloi also?"

"Yes," he said, noticing that she was not fat but medium size.

"How is group farming on your side?"

"We are doing well, in fact some people have planted already," he offered. He noticed that she had put on a short dress over which she wore a *suka* tied at the waist with a long thin piece of cloth.

"Don't you think planting too early like that can ruin the cotton since it is raining too much? We on this side will plant in May when the rains have lessened."

"Yeah, you are right, in fact I personally have not yet planted yet. I am also waiting for May." He fidgeted in his chair, seeing nothing that could tell him that the woman was the witch doctor. Things like goat's feet being worn round the neck, creeping plants tied round the head, wrists and ankles and cowrie shells round the arms, were all missing. So he became more nervous.

"What can I do for you?" Akeso asked, seeing her visitor's discomfort.

"E—r—are you Akeso?"

"What makes you think I am not the one?"

"Well, nothing in particular," Orace replied nervously, trying to smile it off but failing.

"Well," she said, looking far away through the door, "I am Akeso. Now, what can I do for you?" she repeated.

"I just want to know why I am ever having bad luck while a friend of mine always has it good?"

"Eisu!" Akeso called and Eisu appeared in the door way.

"Bring my working things." Eisu disappeared in the bedroom and soon came back with a bag. Akeso went to the left corner of the house and got a small skin of a leopard and placed it in front of her, next to the wall she was facing. She had her back to Orace. Then she got a short stick decorated with cowrie shells whose top was finished off with a bushy tail of a cow. The stick was about one foot long and four inches thick. She stood it against the wall and called Orace to come forward. In front of her, on another skin of a leopard, she emptied different sizes of sea shells. Then she selected small ones — about ten of them and gave them to Orace with both hands and Orace also received them with both hands. Orace sat next to her on her right, also facing the wall.

"Now," she said ,"put those shells next to your mouth and whisper to them all your problems without making me hear. When you have finished talking to them, hand them over to me. Hold them together with two shillings." Orace did as he was told. "I want to know why my daughter died and who killed her," Orace whispered to the shells, his mouth moving like someone praying in church. "Also I want to know why I am always unlucky in everything I do while my friend Okanya gets everything. I want to know what Okanya is using so that you may give me also the same thing. Also I want to know how my remaining children and wife are going to be and if I will enjoy my future. I want to know whether I will be rich one day or if I will die poor," Orace whispered and then gave the shells back to Akeso. When Akeso got the things back, she spat on them and threw them down on the leopard skin. The shells scattered in twos and fours, others in singles.

"Is your mother alive?" she asked.

"No."

"I see a hole on the grave of your mother. It is she who called your daughter. Your daughter entered through that hole to go to her."

Orace listened very attentively. "What may I do about the hole?" he asked.

"Let me see." She collected all the shells, then threw them on the leopard skin again. After that she inspected them for sometime and then said, "You are to get a black goat, kill it, then pour the contents of the intestines into the hole on the grave and return all the stones over the grave. In fact if it is bushy; weed all around it." She got the things again and threw them on the leopard skin. She looked at them for a long time, then straightening said, "My people there," she pointed at the shells, "say there is a man, your neighbour who envies and hates you because of your sons. But he has not bewitched them. They are all alright, even your wife is all right."

"What can I do about that?" Orace asked. He knew now for sure that though Okanya was not his neighbour, he must have been the one jealous and envious of him since he had no sons.

"I will give you the dried head of a chameleon. It is very expensive, you will have to pay 5/=."

"I will pay," Orace said eagerly.

"You are to get pieces of meat from it and make all your children and wife wear them at all times. It diverts the evil's eyes and it makes the evil one slow to act and eventually, giving up any evil action." Akeso again collected the shells and threw them down and then inspected them for a long time after which she straightened saying, "There is nothing more I can see now. You will be okay if you follow what I have been telling you."

Orace was not satisfied so he fidgeted on the animal skin he was sitting on and then said, "I wanted to know why I have been always unlucky."

"It is because of that hole on the grave of your mother. When you have covered it up, you will see."

"Also I wanted to know why a friend of mine is very lucky," Orace said miserably.

"These things of mine cannot answer that question. It needs the person to come and whisper to them for himself and his family only, nobody else."

"In that case, they haven't answered my question about whether I will be rich or die poor," Orace said sullenly.

Akeso burst out laughing." You are a very stubborn man," she said, her eyes still laughing. "You have to work hard and stop drinking or drink little. Then with the seeds I am going to give you to plant in

106

every garden, your crops will never fail you, and you will become rich." That did it. Orace also managed a crooked smile then.

"Bring fifty shillings for ten seeds." Orace gave her the money. She looked into her bag and got out a small tin. She opened the tin and gave him some dried meat she said was from the head of the chameleon. "Let each child and your wife wear it round the neck. Of course you will cut a piece and wrap it in a small cloth. Sew it and put black thread through it for wearing around the necks. You and your big sons can put yours in the pockets of any trousers or shirts you wear."

Orace accepted the meat wrapped in a small paper. He put it in his pocket. Akeso again looked into her bag and fished out another tin, smaller with a black cover. She poured some small red seeds in her hand. She counted ten and returned the rest in the tin.

"Plant these seeds one in each garden. If you have few gardens, keep the rest in a tin with a cover for the future when your children grow up. Plant them in each garden at the eastern corner of the garden. You must plant them during the dry season and never go back to check whether it has germinated or not. You are to forget that you put them there and you must instruct your wife not to work in these gardens when she is having her monthly period. She can walk across them but she must not dig there." She wrapped them too in a small piece of paper and gave it to him. He again put it in his pocket. "That is all for now," she said. "In case of fresh problems, you can of course come back. Now go back and sit there where you have been sitting."

Orace got up painfully and went back to his former position and sat down. He stretched his legs before him, put his hands on his head and stretched his body, yawning, causing his eyes to water. He felt better, much better. Akeso collected her things, put them back in the bag, then returned them to the bedroom. She came back to the sitting room and sat on the mat.

"Eisu!" she called. "Where are you? He should come and go to buy beer for the visitor. Eisu!"

"Don't worry," Orace put in quickly, "I will take it next time. I have a lot of work at home and it is still early, anyway. Beer taken early causes a headache."

"It is bad seeing a visitor go back with his very saliva only!" she moaned. She had no intentions of buying beer but was just pretending. It was her trick to make people think her hospitable. If Eisu had been present, she would have sent him and at her instructions, he would have reported back that the brew was 'young' so that the visitor would still leave without taking beer.

"I am leaving," Orace said at last.

"Okay, but it is sad you didn't eat anything."

"It is all right," Orace said.

"Now please don't say good bye to me and don't look back. Just get up, get your bicycle then go and don't branch to anybody's home." That was what Orace did. When he arrived at home, he told his wife about everything and she straightaway started to sew as directed. The whole day Orace stayed at home, which was very unusual because he never missed a day without drinking. I am going to ask Okanya one day why he is ever lucky, he told himself.

Chapter Fifteen

Two days after the visitors left Okanya's place, Abeso and Anaro
started to prepare beer so that when Ewiu's people came for
Anaro, after three weeks, the beer would be ready. Abeso and
her daughter threshed millet and filled four large baskets. The millet
was mixed with water in one corner of the kitchen and left to ferment
for two days. On the third day it was put out to dry, after which it was
ground. They worked together while Abeso continued to educate
Anaro. "Now Anna," Abeso said, "you will be the one to prepare this
beer, after all, it will be for the last time."

"That is okay, mother," Anaro said. Abeso made a large hole with a
circumference of about two feet and about two feet deep. Then using
the banana leaves, she covered the bottom and the sides of the hole.
Anaro swept the kitchen verandah next to the hole, then she brought
the fermented millet and poured it down where she had swept. She
also brought a pot of water and a calabash and placed them near the
place of work. When she had finished to arrange these things, she
knelt in front of the millet, ready to start mixing.

"I am ready, mother," she called. Abeso came over, and then Anaro
made a hole in the middle of the millet flour with her hand and Abeso
poured water into it. Anaro then, with the right hand, mixed a small
paste and licked it and then with the same hand she touched some of
the paste with her temples, then blowing out the millet in her mouth,
she said, "Bitter, bitter, be bitter like *opong* and may those who drink
you get drunk and fight."

"Don't say fight," Abeso said, laughing. "It can happen.Of course it will not make them fight, but it will make them so drunk that they will feel like fighting. Only they will be too weak to fight."

They were just talking because that was the procedure. Sometimes people could drink and fight, at times not. Abeso continued to pour water while Anaro did the mixing, using both hands. When the whole of it was properly mixed, Anaro got a large calabash and with it she dished out the paste and poured it in the hole already prepared with banana leaves. When the hole was half full, Anaro pressed down the paste all around, especially the sides. When all the paste in the hole had been pressed hard, Anaro covered it. She then washed her hands over the brew, after which she covered the whole thing with banana leaves. Then she used the soil dug out of the hole to make mud to cement it. She returned all the remaining soil, dug out of the hole, on top of the brew, using a hoe. After that, Abeso sprinkled water over it and Anaro beat gently all around it, using grass and a stick. That done, Anaro went out and cut a thorny branch of a tree which she put over it so that chickens or goats would not disturb it.

"What is the date today?" Abeso asked.

"It is the 1st of May."

"Good," Abeso said. "We will fry the beer on the 14th and those people will come for you on the 21st. That is good."

No one has ever found out why time flies when one is busy! Everyday Okanya went to his cotton garden to dig where the plough had missed. He was so intent on finishing the patches that he didn't realise how quickly the day for his daughter to leave home was drawing near. As usual, they discussed things at night in bed.

"We fried the beer today," Abeso told her husband. "And the weather has been kind to us. I think the last heavy rain must have been for washing the face of the moon."

"Yes," Okanya agreed. He was feeling so tired, his back ached.

"We have a few days left how," Abeso reminded him hesitantly.

"So?" Okanya said.

"Well, what are we going to cook for the visitors?"

"That he-goat has to go, I have nothing to do." They had only one goat.

110

"And hoping that the women around will bring us food too, I think it will be okay."

"Last time I was so excited I bought too much dry fish and I spent all the money I had," Okanya said. "And you saw the amount of food that was left-over. It was too much," he concluded.

"Well, I just wanted to make sure about that," Abeso said.

"How many days are left?" he asked.

"Only four."

"Then you should inform the women tomorrow so that they can start brewing beer."

"Yes, I will do that."

"Sure, do it tomorrow so that they bring *kongo polwo*. You know that *kongo ira*. causes a headache and *polwo* makes one drunk quickly. That is what they want." And it was and still is true. When one drinks and does not get drunk at a marriage ceremony, he does not consider it a success. People want to get drunk, fall off their bicycles and do all sorts of weird things drunks do in order to feel they have enjoyed themselves. So Okanya wanted to make the brew so tough so that his visitors would drink and get drunk and say, "Oh that party at Okanya's was great and well organized; we drank so much."

So the following day Abeso once more went from home to home, telling women to put their fried beer in water, so that the visitors would drink it on its 4th day as *kongo polwo*. *Kongo irra* is drank on the 3rd day and the *abisi*, the very sweet one and a favourite of children, is taken on the 2nd day. The last one is very sweet and satisfying but it causes headache, and from time to time you belch and pass hot air form the stomach via the nose, breaking it, so to speak.

The days passed quickly and soon it was Saturday, the day for Anaro to leave home. She had washed her dresses and packed them in her small wooden yellow box. She gave Ikiso her blanket. Okanya put fresh dry grass on the floor of the *goga* and Abeso brought old sacks and papyrus mats and spread them over the grass. The *goga* of the previous ceremony was still standing so Okanya didn't have to build another one. He had some young boys bring chairs and tables from neighbours. The goat was slaughtered and was on fire in one cooking place. Another had a large saucepan of water, still cold. Two

111

drums of water stood by. The water was collected by young women and girls of the clan. After fetching the water, they ran back to their homes to bathe and put on their best clothes to receive the visitors.

Abeso swept both houses. They were clean, and the floors freshly smeared with cow dung. All her pots were covered and all the plates, including borrowed ones, cups and calabashes were put outside on the *tandalo*. She washed four large pots and put them out to dry. Ikiso's bed was taken to their bedroom because the kitchen was full of pots of beer, of all sizes. Women came carrying pots of beer on their heads and their little girls carrying saucepans of food.

Okanya prepared the straw tubes, and tested them to make sure they were okay. The leaking ones were sealed off by winding thread around them and smearing barsoap over the thread. The mouths of the tubes were cleaned and trimmed off with a razor blade. That done, Okanya arranged chairs in the *goga*..

The *goga* this time was separated into four parts. Each part had a hole dug in the middle of it for putting the pot of beer. Only two parts had chairs and tables. Okanya divided it in four parts because the visitors would sit, with men on chairs in one part and their women in another part, sitting on papyrus mats. That was one half of the *goga*. The other half for clansmen and women was arranged in the same manner. The clans people would share pots of beer with Abeso's relatives. Then there was a fifth group called *Iwanyaki*. These people were usually uninvited and were expected to leave before the visitors.

After Okanya had arranged the *goga*, he took a bath and put on his light blue long-sleeved shirt, a black pair of trousers and a pair of new black shoes bought with part of his share of the dowry. He combed his hair and went to the *goga*. Esemu, his friend, was already there. They shook hands and sat down. Esemu was wearing a secondhand black pair of trousers and a yellow short-sleeved shirt and rubber sandals.

"Anaro," Okanya called and she came. "Tell your mother to bring us something. We can't just sit here doing nothing while we wait," Okanya said, looking at his friend who smiled. Anaro took the message and her mother gave her a mall pot of beer which she took to her father and his friend. The water was boiling so she put some in a

112

calabash for pouring in her father's beer. He started drinking with Esemu while they talked.

Abeso also took a bath, put on her flowered *gomas* and tied her head with a white head-dress which had the picture of Pope Paul the 6th on one side and Prime Minister Obote on the other. She did not put on any footwear because she was going to run up and down and she could do it better on her bare feet. Anaro also took a bath and put on her blue twist dress and blue slippers. She oiled and combed her hair. With her friend Lilly, she sat inside the big house where some chairs and a mat had been arranged in a circle. The room was clean, all pots covered. Thus ready, they waited for the visitors to come.

The sun was starting to be hot. The sky was cloudless and blue, probably in answer to Abeso's prayers. Rain was the last thing she wanted that day. The clans people came and were given places to sit. Then as people were becoming less talkative and anxious, the visitors came. Ewiu came on a bicycle with his friend William Okwapa. They were both smartly dressed in trousers, shoes and long-sleeved white shirts. They were relieved of their bicycle. Then Okanya led them to his own house, where the bride and groom would sit. A young woman of the clan was appointed to look after the bride and groom with their group which consisted of young boys and girls like Okwapa and Lilly, and some young married couples. When all were seated, Okanya organised boys to distribute food on plates. The boys took the food first to Ewiu's uncle who ate alone while his people shared plates of vegetables and millet bread in twos and threes. Next, food was taken to Ewiu's group. There were boys who distributed the food while others followed with a basin and water for washing hands. The plates were not enough, so the visitors ate while the clans people sat, awaiting their turn to eat. After the visitors had all eaten, some boys collected the plates while others followed with soap and water for washing hands. After that, pots of beer were put in front of the visitors, tubes distributed and hot water poured.

After that the clans people and the *Iwanyaki* ate and after the plates were cleared they too were given pots of beer.

The place was noisy. People were talking all at once and the noise could be heard from two miles away. Everywhere there was the

113

smell of meat and beer. Abeso put Esemu's wife in charge of the distribution of beer. So when everyone had a pot of beer, she locked the kitchen and kept the key. Her work was to visit every group from time to time to see if their beer was till 'strong'. Abeso went and sat chatting for a long time, making jokes with the women of Ewiu's clan. Okanya did the same with the men but their group went on drinking for a long time and later started to dance within their groups.

The sun was moving towards the west. It had left the middle of the sky, making shadows long. The bitterness had gone out of it. A good time for chickens to come out of the bush to eat any grain spread out to dry. A time when co-women abused each other indirectly, using the chickens. That was the time Amolo, a young woman of Ewiu's clan, called Anaro to come out so that they could see her.

"Our wife, where are you? Come and we see you," she called. People were talking loudly but those in Okanya's house heard.

"They are calling you," Ewiu told Anaro.

"Lilly, let us go," Anaro said, starting to panic. She was feeling nervous but the beer she had been taking made her a bit bold. They went out and greeted the women and men of Ewiu's clan. They were drunk but all were eager to see what type of woman they were soon to include in their clan. Their searching eyes made Anaro shy so that she talked looking down most of the time. When she had greeted everybody she went back to Amolo who took her to the *sakaite* (bathroom). Two young women were already there with water in a basin and soap. There was a wooden box in one dry corner of the *sakaite*.

"Now my daughter," Amolo told Lilly, "leave us alone. We want to bathe our wife." Lilly went back to the house. Ewiu was being introduced to Anaro's clans people. Meanwhile, Anaro was feeling too shy to undress in front of these women. "Don't fear," Amolo reasured her. "It is the custom; all of us here had to be bathed before we were brought to join the clan of our husbands." So Anaro gained courage and stripped. They bathed her whole body, leaving only her head which had long hair that would take too long to dry. When they had finished bathing her and oiling her rounded breasts, firm buttocks, legs, and the rest of her with baby jelly, they got out a *gomas*, a knicker, a petticoat and *kikoyi* (under garment) and helped her to dress since this was her first time to put on such garments. Then they combed her hair and sprinkled powder between her breasts. They got out brown shoes and made her put them on. Then they folded the dress and underwear which she had been wearing and put them in their suitcase, together with her slippers. They covered her head with a three metre long white cloth. Thus clothed, she left the bathroom, walking very slowly with the other women.

When the people in the *goga* saw them, women ululated and people began to sing and dance. Once inside, she was made to sit in the chair next to Ewiu. Then Anaro covered both of them with the white cloth. Women clapped. A fresh pot of beer was put in front of them and the rest of the people. Then Anaro was given a tube which she shared with Ewiu only. They drank and got up to dance. They danced slowly within the sheet. After that they sat down together.

"Where is your sister today?" Ewiu asked.

"She is around but I don't know where," Anaro answered. They talked softly. Someone was told to go and call Ikiso. She came shyly and knelt near her sister and greeted everybody. "I am taking you sister," Ewiu said.

"It is all right," Ikiso answered, managing a weak smile. She was near tears.

"That is good. Here, buy something with that," Ewiu said giving her 100/=. People around them clapped and laughed. They were all merry.

"Thank you," Ikiso said and fled to her parents' bedroom. She could not manage to say 'bye' to her sister.

Shortly after that Okanya came in and he was given a seat. "Anaro my daughter, you are now going. Don't shame us in front of my in-laws. Go in peace and may the Lord keep you and bless you with many children." Everyone was quiet, then turning to Ewiu Okanya said, "My son, I wish you well and please look after my daughter well. I have given her to you in good condition. May the Lord keep her, with your help, always healthy."

Ewiu got up and shook Okanya's hand smiling. "I will do that," he said and sat down. Okanya left and Abeso came in. She sat on a mat facing the couple. She was not miserable: she was happy but not very happy at this parting. Anaro had been her favourite.

"I have nothing to say," she said. "I only ask the Lord to bless you with many children and may you live peacefully together!" The women clapped and she went out.

Outside was not as cool as inside had been. Two young boys were fighting and people were busy trying to separate them. "What happened?" Abeso asked the nearest person.

"I don't know either. You know, this beer of yours is very strong and those boys thought it was little so they took it at a high speed. That is the trouble." Abeso was not disturbed. She saw Okanya standing there trying to settle the problem. It was the boys of Ewiu's clan who were fighting. When Anaro was making beer, she had said, "Bitter, bitter, be so bitter so that people may drink you and get drunk and fight." Abeso remembered it and she smiled to herself. The problem was settled and the two shook hands and were brothers once again.

Beer continued to flow. The sun had gone west where it cast cold golden rays. It was called *onyek mon* (the jealousy of women) because it was sometimes used by the older co-wife to deceive the younger one. She would say, "Escort me to the well." The younger one would say, "But I have not yet put food on the fire and our husband will soon be home." "But look at the sun, it is still there," the elder woman would insist and they would go. But by the time they reached the well, the sun would be gone and the cows would be on their way home. And when the husband came home, the food would not be ready and the wife would be in trouble.

It was at this stage that Ebwonyu thanked Okanya and all his clans people and told his clans people that they should get ready to leave. A special bicycle with a capable rider, one who looked less drunk, was chosen. This man then rolled the bicycle up to the door step of Okanya's house. He sat on the bicycle with his back to the house, ready to take off. When the women inside saw it, they started singing, drumming, clapping and making ululations in between. They sang:

Otero, Otero, Oter, mugole Otero turwa.
Solo - kiton dyang da Okwanyo!
Chorus - otero mugole Otero turwa

Sol - kiton kongo da konyobo!
Chr - otero mugole otero turwa
Sol - iton dek da kotedo
Chr - otero —, otero!
Chr - otero mugole otero turwa.

The women sang the above song continuously while drumming and clapping as they escorted Anaro and Ewiu out of the house. Okwapa also brought his bicycle and sat on it near the first man. Anaro went and sat on the bicycle of the first man. Amolo covered her head properly with a white sheet. And thus ready, the rider took off amid cheers, ululations, alarms, singing and dancing.

When Anaro and her rider disappeared from view, Okwapa also rode off with Ewiu sitting on the bicycle carrier. This time women just sang and waved. No ululations or alarms for men.

After the couple had left, Ewiu's people followed, most of them on foot. Those who had come on bicycles were too drunk to ride. So they simply rolled them along as they shouted their goodbyes until they were hidden from view.

After seeing off the visitors, Okanya's people went back back to the *goga* where fresh pots of beer were put before them. The *iwanyak* were also given a fresh pot of beer. Okanya went to them and said, "Now, friends, I am glad you came but I must ask you kindly to leave after finishing the pot we have just given you."

"It is all right. We are very grateful to you," they replied.

"It is a shame telling you to go but that is because there is no more beer. But don't worry, there will be other times." After that Okanya rejoined his people and they drank until almost dawn. The clans people then left and Okanya and his wife continued to drink until sunrise.

117

Chapter Sixteen

That was May, the month Anaro left home to join her husband, Joseph Ewiu. That very month Okanya planted his cotton. Ikiso continued with her schooling and Abeso also continued to visit Nurse Rose about the pills she was taking. One day she noticed clots in her monthly blood flow. This worried her as it had never happened before. Could it be the European medicine she was taking? if that was so, she would rather have her period twice a month than once with clots. So she set out for Lwala Hospital and went straight to Nurse Rose's ward. Rose spotted her standing uneasily at the entrance of the ward and beckoned her in. "You are welcome," she said smiling.

"Thank you. But I am interrupting your work," Abeso said, sitting down on a chair.

"That is okay. By the way, thanks again for inviting me to the party. I enjoyed myself very much. You must have brewed a lot of beer. Has Anaro been taken yet?"

"Yes, she was taken last week," Abeso told her.

"Is she still at home or has she gone to join Ewiu in Kampala?"

"He has taken her to Kampala."

"You must be lonely without her."

"Yes, I am lonely but I am worried about something else. That is why I have come to see you," Abeso said.

"Tell me about it," Nurse Rose said sympathetically.

"I think it is the European medicine you gave me which is making me sick," Abeso said.

118

"How does it make you sick?" Nurse Rose asked, getting impatient. But she knew that hurrying her would not do and made herself wait while Abeso uncovered her illness, step by step.

"My monthly period came two days ago," Abeso said. Nurse Rose waited. "When I used to be sick twice or three times a month, the bleeding used to be light. Now it has clots."

"Are the clots big?" Murse Rose asked.

"They are the size of small stones," Abeso replied, looking worried.

"How many days does it take?"

"It takes four days but it is the clots that worry me. I want to stop swallowing these European medicines."

Nurse Rose thought for some time and then said, "Okay. You can stop taking the medicine. Stop for one month and then come and see me. If you continue to bleed three times a month, then I will take you to Soroti Hospital to see a doctor."

"Thank you very much," Abeso said, relieved.

"Don't mention it," Rose replied. "If Anaro comes back from Kampala, please tell her to come and see me."

"I will tell her. She is taking only two months there, since the harvest season will soon be starting. She will then come back to prepare beer so that our people can go to see the cows," Abeso said, getting up. "I was so woried I did not bring you even mangoes," she added, looking embarrassed.

"That is all right," Rose answered and smiled. "Do you have to bring me something each time you come to see me?" She escorted her up to the main road, and then went back.

Abeso felt better. She would leave those medicines alone now. She had been wise in going to see Rose before the days of swallowing began. She hurried along the lonely road. She could tell from the shadows and the position of the sun that it was nearing noon. She saw ripe mangoes in the bush and branched off. The mango tree was tall with branches weighted downwards with mangoes. Some were ripe, others just beginning to ripen and yet others still green. Abeso looked for a stick and knocked down many mangoes. Then using her headscarf, she gathered them in it, tied it and carried the bundle on her head and left. She met nobody on the main road . She ate her mangoes one by one as she walked.

June came and went and in July the millet harvest started. Theirs was a type of millet which could grow very well but took too long to ripen. Oyuru, Okanya's brother who had planted *ekama* had already eaten *agwee* (new millet). The work involved was great. Harvesting the millet, then spreading it out to dry and eventually putting it in the granary. Okanya only helped with the harvesting. The rest of the work was done by Abeso alone. In addition, she had to cook, go to the well for water, grind millet, collet fire wood, and so on. So it was not any wonder she did not realise she had missed her monthly periods until months later! Okanya had noticed it but had said nothing about it. Usually Abeso moved down to sleep on a mat when she was having her periods but for almost two months now, she had not done so! What was the matter? Could she be pregnant? Abeso was not yet forty years but with their last born in P.7, how could it be possible? Okanya was disturbed. He turned and changed position several times so that Abeso would wake up, but she didn't. He had noticed also that Abeso slept quickly and very deeply those days. He turned and rolled to make Abeso aware of him but Abeso instead changed her position and fell asleep again. He let her sleep but he was worried. He had to talk to her. They slept, then towards the middle of the night, Abeso woke up. She yawned and went out to pass urine. That was also new. Abeso usually passed urine once before going to bed till morning. She came back and climbed the bed cautiously so as not to awake her husband but Okanya said, "When are you moving down?"

"Down where?" Abeso inquired sleepily. Then she remembered and the sleep disappeared.

"My moon is lost!" she said.

"Where have you lost it?" Okanya teased.

"I don't know, but I don't think I'm pregnant. If I were pregnant, I would have started vomiting and hating you and certain foods."

"Good," Okanya smiled in the darkness.

"What is good?" Abeso wanted to know. "Suppose it is *arugude* (fibroids)?"

120

"That is why I am saying good. If it is *arugude*, I will marry a second wife."

Anger rose in Abeso. She sat up. "You wouldn't dare marry a second wife with my daughter's cows!"

"Like a shot I would. Most men have two to three homes."

"But they don't bring women with their children's cows," Abeso argued tearfully.

"They do," Okanya said.

Abeso had feared the very thing Okanya was saying now. At one time, Okanya had talked only about buying a car and starting business if he had money. She had felt pleased then. It must have been that quarrel he had with Orace about having no son which had made him change his mind. Abeso covered her face with both her hands and rocked with misery. A second wife and with my very daughters's cows! Oh, I wish I had a son. It wouldn't happen like this. My son would bring a woman with his sister's cows. Now Okanya is going to bring a woman who can produce sons and her sons will also marry with my daughter's cows, then I will stop existing. What did I do to the spirits of my grandparents? Okanya, though cruel, has been a good husband, maybe because he was poor. Soon he will be rich with my daughter's cows and where will I be? She started crying silently but of course she had to blow her nose, so Okanya realised that he had annoyed her. Women, he thought, a small thing and it is tears!

"Assistant," he called, pulling her towards him on the bed. Abeso lay down slowly still crying, swallowing loudly.

"Now why should you cry just because I mentioned a second wife?" Okanya spoke kindly to her. He felt great. Few women would cry for him. He always knew Abeso loved him very much. Hadn't she proved it that time when she came back to him after that terrible beating he had given her? In fact he had not expected her to come back to him, yet she had come. Was that not true love? I must try to be nice to this woman, Okanya told himself. She loves me, that is why she is crying. I will never beat her again! She is true to me. Aloud he said, "Assistant, don't cry. You are no long a child and I was just joking." He pulled her towards him and put his arms around her. "I am not rich yet," he continued, "and Ewiu can still decide to send our daughter back. Don't

121

you remember Orace's daughter's case? You shouldn't worry unnecessarily. Even if I were to marry, do you think I would forget you? And who wants two women, anyway? Always quarrelling, making a man eat all the rubbish and dirt they collect! Now seriously, what are we going to do about your monthly sickness?"

Abeso blew her nose, wiped her eyes with the blanket and said, "I am going to see Nurse Rose first."

"Yes, do that," Okanya said. "If after seeing her there is no pregnancy and no period, then I will have to take you to see a witch doctor. Could be the spirits of my parents are annoyed with us. In fact I always thought that they could be the ones who 'tied your uterus' too early. You are not yet old and yet you have already stopped giving birth. Look at Ebwoyu's wife. Do you know him?" Abeso nodded. "His wife has just given birth to their tenth child, yet her hair is turning white!"

"But do you think I can be pregnant?" Abeso asked after a long pause.

"Of course," he said, turning on his back. "Haven't I just told you about Ebwoyu's wife? She is old yet she is now breastfeeding. You cannot be her age-mate. Where is your white hair?"

Abeso kept quiet for sometime and then said, "If I am to go to the hospital, then you will help me and spread the millet out to dry. The millet we brought in yesterday. It is in one corner of the kitchen."

"Can't you do that when you come back?" Okanya asked. "I am going to start weeding my cotton garden."

"How do I know how long I am going to take there? If that millet is not brought out to dry tomorrow, it is going to start germinating."

"All right," Okanya agreed. "Then prepare me something to eat before you go." After that they slept till morning. Abeso got up first and after preparing some food for Okanya, left for Lwala Hospital.

"Good morning," Abeso greeted the nurse she found in the room where she always met Nurse Rose. "Where is Nurse Rose?"

"She hasn't come yet. Have a seat while I go and call her." Abeso sat on her usual chair, in the white examination room with a large crucifix. After about thirty minutes, Nurse Rose came in wearing an ordinary dress instead of a uniform.

122

"Good morning. Sorry I kept you waiting."

"Good morning," Abeso answered. "I should be the one to apologise for disturbing you so early in the morning."

"That is okay," Rose said. "I would have come as soon as the other nurse came for me but I was not there. I had gone to get some water down in the village. Now tell me, what happened? I waited for you the whole of last month but you didn't come."

"Sure I didn't come," Abeso said. "We have been so busy harvesting millet that I didn't notice a month had passed."

"I see," Rose said. "How are you getting on?"

"Very badly," Abeso said mournfully. Nurse Rose looked at her more carefully. She looked healthier, even fatter. Now what could have happened? She waited patiently for her to answer. "I haven't seen my 'monthly sickness' again since I stopped swallowing those European medicines you gave me. In fact since I left here the other month, I haven't been sick."

"Good," Nurse Rose said excitedly. Abeso felt confused. Was it good not to see your 'monthly sickness' when you know it cannot be pregnancy?

"Come and lie on this bed and take off your clothes. I am going to examine you." Nurse Rose closed the door and window, then rubbed her hands together for about two minutes before she started to palpate Abeso's abdomen. She also checked the eyes for anaemia, inspected the feet for any signs of oedema, saw her nails and hands. She discovered that Abeso was seven weeks pregnant. "Put on your clothes," she said at length. When Abeso had put on her dress and sat down, Nurse Rose said simply, "My friend, you are going to have a baby. You are pregnant." Abeso's heart jumped with those words, sending blood to her head.

"Is it true?" She couldn't believe it.

"Yes," Nurse Rose said. "Why can't it be true?"

"How can it be," Abeso wondered aloud, "when my last born, Ikiso is in P.7?"

Nurse Rose laughed. "It does not matter how old the last born is. It is your age that matters. You are still within the age of child bearing," she explained.

123

"Then what had happened to me?" Abeso asked.

"I don't know. It must have been the irregularity of your monthly periods responsible for your inability to conceive. Didn't you tell me you used to be sick three times a month?"

"Yes," Abeso said still not convinced.

"Those European medicines helped to make your monthly sickness regular and when you stopped taking them, they had already cured you, so you conceived. Are you happy?"

"Of course I am happy," Abeso said. "It is only that I had stopped hoping for another child, that is why I am like this."

"I am happy for you, my friend," Rose said. "You must now come back on Wednesday with fifteen shilling so that you can start taking more European medicine to maintain the baby. Do you understand?"

"Yes," Abeso said.

"Let us go home for breakfast, I had not yet taken mine," Rose invited.

They went to Nurse Rose's house and had tea with roasted groundnuts and then Abeso left. All the way home, her head was busy with unbelieving thoughts. Could Nurse Rose have deceived her? Not likely. Anyway, she consoled herself, I have been pregnant before and I know the signs. I will believe it when the child starts moving in my abdomen; but then they say that even *arugude* moves, makes the breasts big and the abdomen to swell. But the worst part is that I don't vomit! I will tell nurse Rose about it when we meet next. If this was a child, I would be vomiting because with my two girls, I always vomited in the morning. Unless of course if I were carrying a boy. Carrying a boy! She stopped short in her steps. 'Oh! God let it be so,' she prayed. She branched in the bush for some mangoes, collected them in her headscarf and continued her journey home, eating one by one.

Okanya had finished to spread the millet. He was starting to eat when he saw his wife coming, eating a mango. Abeso put the remaining mangoes in a basket then got a mat and went with it outside to the verandah where her husband was.

"How did it go?" he asked anxiously when Abeso had sat down.

"The nurse said I am pregnant," Abeso announced.

124

Okanya kept quiet and prayed silently, 'Please God, let it be a boy.'
"How did she know?" he asked at length.

"She examined me."

"What else did she say?"

"She said that I must go back on Wednesday with fifteen shillings so that I can start drinking European medicine to maintain the baby."

"I see," Okanya said doubtfully.

"I told her it could not be," Abeso continued, "because you know how big Ikeso, our last born is."

"Yes. Ikiso is thirteen now."

"She insisted that the age of the last born does not matter. She said that it is my age that matters. She said I cannot be 40 years old, therefore I am still in the child bearing age."

"Then what must have happened?" Okanya asked the same question Abeso had asked Nurse Rose.

"My 'monthly sickness' was the cause. It was not steady. You remember how I used to sleep down sometimes three times a month?"

"I remember."

"Well," Abeso continued, "they worried me so I went and told Nurse Rose about it and she gave me some European medicines to swallow. I have been swallowing them ever since, then two months ago, I started bleeding with clots, so I went back and told Nurse Rose about it. She advised me to stop the medicines and so when I stopped, this happened."

"You mean it was only the 'monthly sickness' holding back all those children I should have had?"

"It would seem so because as soon as the sickness became steady, I conceived."

They ate together, then Okanya went to bed to rest. He wanted to think of this new development. Abeso changed and started going about the routine of sweeping houses, cleaning, fetching water and preparing supper. She was happy! If only it could be so. Then Okanya would not bring a second woman because he had wanted to do so in order to have more children.

Chapter Seventeen

August was the best month of the year. It was and still is a month of eating and drinking. It is the month when groundnuts are harvested and beer parties for revenging back are held. A month when children look healthier with occasional loose stool due to eating too much raw and roasted groundnuts. A month when cows are slaughtered and the meat exchanged with millet. A month of rejoicing and occasional sorrow caused by young boys and men who fight at beer parties, but still August remains a very good month, in fact a better month for lazy people. Because by August, all the millet is harvested, cotton already planted, beans ready to eat, potatoes, as big as a fat child's arm, all ready. A month when house wives look cleaner, go to the markets more often, brew beer for sale and for husbands. What about the man, the head of family; what does August bring him? What else but rest. Attending beer parties; supervising his children in his cotton garden, if he has children, because it is also in August when school children come back home for the second term holidays.

For young girls and boys, August is a month for courtship, when many dances are held. *Okembe* and record player dances. A month when rains are less, the sky more blue and the moon at night, which lights up the whole heaven. And for couples getting married, August is the best because it is a month of plenty when neighbours can afford to be generous.

That is why Ewiu chose August to send Anaro back home to prepare beer for her people, so that her cows could be seen and taken, the sealing of marriage.

Anaro used *Saa-Mbaya* bus and by 4.30 p.m she was already at Lwala shops. She carried the little luggage she had on her head. Lwala looked empty to her since she was now used to seeing many people and cars in Kampala. She had not gone far when ahead she saw school children. She clapped her hands and all of them looked behind. One of the children detached herself and ran towards her. It was Ikiso. She ran jumping and smiling.

"Anna, Anna, Anna!" she cried over and over again. She put her arms around her sister, then after sometime she took over the luggage which Anaro was carrying.

"How is everybody at home?"

"They are all right except that mother is pregnant."

"Is that so!" Anaro said not believing.

"It is so."

"Oh dear," she laughed. "I am so glad to hear it. Ikiso, are you not pleased? You are going to be *nyapid* proper.

"But 1 am in school," Ikiso said.

"How is father?"

"He is okay; his cotton is doing well. Mother prepared beer then people came to help him weed."

"How nice!"

"But how is Kampala? You are looking smart and fatter, what do people there eat?"

"They eat what people here also eat except that it is so big and so nice. One day I will take you to see it."

"Sure?" Ikiso asked smiling, her eyes growing round with pleasure. Thus chatting, they reached the junction where they separated.

"Tell mother I am coming there tomorrow," Anaro said and went her way. Ikiso ran all the way home. She was so excited. She found her mother sitting on a mat under the *akulong* tree in front of their house. "What can I tell you mother?" Ikiso shouted without preliminaries. "Anaro is back! She said that she is coming here tomorrow."

"Where did you meet her?" her mother inquired happily.

127

"On the road from school. We were in front, she clapped her hands and when we looked behind, there she was."

"How is she?"

"Mother, she is looking clean, fat and smart."

"That is good. Did she say when Ewiu would also come?"

"I didn't ask her about that."

"Good. Food is in the kitchen, eat and then go to the well. I was feeling lazy today I didn't fetch water." Ikiso went into the kitchen to do as she was told.

"Change your uniform before you start eating," Abeso shouted after her.

In the evening when they were having supper, Ikiso took her report to her father.

"Second term has ended today, father, here is the report." Ikiso knelt down and gave her father the report.

"What was your position?"

"I was the 7th out of 35 pupils."

"Try harder," Okanya said without opening the report.

Ikiso laughed.

"What is it?" her father asked.

"I was remembering what happened to one of the children last term."

"What happened to the child?"

"She was the first in P.1, but when she went home and told her father her position, he became very angry with her and beat her and after that he brought her to school, still quarrelling about her position which he mistook for her marks. 'Other children get a hundred and you waste my money getting only one!' "

"Hm, what happened then?" Okanya asked.

"He wanted to know if his daughter was attending school. How could she get only one if she attended school."

"What did the teachers do?"

"They explained to him the meaning of numbers, then he went back home. He was feeling very embarrassed, but the children up to today call that girl number one."

"What number did you say you got?"

"Number seven."

"Yeah, it is going to be my turn to take you to your teachers. How will you get grade 'A' with that number?" Okanya was angry and his anger wiped off the humour that had been hovering on all their faces. Ikiso's heart sunk and she started sweating.

"We are going to talk about this report tomorrow. It is already dark, I can't read it."

After sometime, Abeso broke the silence and said, "Ikiso tells me that Anna came back today."

"Where did she meet her?"

"On the road from school."

"That is good," Okanya said, his mind shifting, easing the tension.

"She is coming to see us tomorrow," Abeso went on. Ikiso, seeing that her father's attention was diverted, got up and left the room silently without a word to anyone.

"Oh, just tomorrow?" Okanya complained. "Then we have to buy her beer, when it would have been better if you had brewed."

"Yes," Abeso agreed. "But I am sure she will understand. I am sure she wants to see us briefly before she goes to prepare the beer at Kakeno."

"I know," Okanya said. "But Ewiu's mother must have prepared half of it by now."

"I wouldn't doubt it. She is a very reasonable woman."

"She is," Okanya agreed. They talked for sometime and then they went to bed.

***

The following day was a Saturday. The sun rose slowly from the east, bathing the trees, grass, and houses with its golden rays, and casting small irregular shadows here and there. Anaro got up early. She went to the well three times, of course taking the water to Lakeri's house. After that she prepared breakfast and after breakfast, announced her imminent visit.

"I am going home, mother." A good girl never mentions the name of her mother-in-law. Instead she simply calls her 'mother'.

"When will you be back?"

"I'll come back after two days."

'I know you want to be with your people but are you not back because of some preparations?"

"Yes, mother."

"In that case," the wise old woman continued, "I will expect you on Sunday evening. We have to go to Kakeno on Monday. I have been there preparing beer with the help of my co-wives. We have left you two tins to prepare. The millet is already dry, so all you have to do is grind, bury and fry."

"Thank you mother. I thought the millet was not yet fermented. Oh, that is very kind of you mother," Anaro said with a smile. The old woman also smiled, calling more wrinkles to her face.

"That is okay, my daughter. Now run along home and greet everybody there for me." So Anaro left.

Ikiso was brooding on the verandah, expecting her father to call her about the school report when she saw her sister coming. She forgot everything and ran to meet her. "You are welcome, you are welcome." Abeso heard Ikiso's shouts of joy and knew that it must be her other daughter, Anna Anaro, and came out smiling broadly. She had put on a dress with tiny gathers at the waist.

"You are welcome home," Abeso shouted. Presently Anaro and Ikiso entered the house, holding hands. Abeso had prepared the papyrus mat for sitting on, so Anaro went straight to it, her face wreathed in smiles. She sat down, remembering to kick off her slippers. Ikiso hovered about as though she expected her mother and sister to eat each other but nothing of that sort happened. Abeso was talking all the time before she sat down.. "Kampala people, we never expected you back so soon." She sat down, then both of them shook hands for a long time. Abeso was looking into her daughter's eyes all the time, as though trying to read something in them. "How is it there?" she asked.

"It is all right."

"You are welcome home," she repeated.

"I am glad to see you too."

"As I greet you, I am even feeling ashamed," Abeso said, dropping her daughter's hands. "Look at me," she said looking at her abdomen.

"At my age, with my elder daughter married!"

"But mother, you are still young and I am your first born. If I had been your last born and you were like this, then I would worry," Anaro said and looked around her as though expecting a lot of changes. But nothing had changed, except her mother whose skin was becoming lighter, and looking younger.

"You are looking well and I forget, is this the *gomas* in which you were taken from here?"

"No, mother, he bought me this one from Kampala," Anaro answered. Then Ikiso came and sat near her and fingered the material. Abeso also fingered it. "It is called *mafuta*," Anaro explained the texture of the material.

"*Mafuta?*" Abeso and Ikiso querried together.

"Yes, it is called m*afuta* because it is very expensive. People with *mafuta*, I mean, rich people only can afford to buy it. That's what I was told."

"Ewiu must be a big police officer then."

"He tells me that he is a corporal."

"What uniform does a corporal wear?" Abeso asked.

"They wear the same uniform except that on his right sleeve of the uniform, he pins two *chepes*. Where is father?"

Abeso looked out before answering. "There he comes. He had gone to buy you some beer from Esemu's place. But he delayed there. He went early before the sun was up and look at the sun now, it must be ten o'clock." Then turning to Ikiso she said, "Ikiso, go and run after that chicken, *aokosen*, you know the one." Ikiso left to go and catch the chicken. Okanya put the bicycle behind the house then came in carrying a medium sized pot of beer. Abeso got up to get it from him saying; "Why did you take so long? Did you drink a bit from there?" Okanya ignored her. He got a chair and sat near his daughter. Anaro got up and knelt to greet her father.

"You are welcome home," he said.

" I am glad to see you, father," Anaro replied.

"How was the journey?"

"It was all right." Both were smiling happily. While they were still talking, Abeso came with a small pot of beer and two tubes, plus an old hardware plate. She put the plate down in front of Anaro who got the tubes from her, then put the pot on the plate.

"Ikiso!" Abeso called. They could hear Ikiso's footsteps, running after the chicken. "She hasn't caught it yet!" she said, going to the kitchen to collect hot water.

Okanya got out of the house. "Ikiso," he called. "Spit saliva after it while running. It makes it tire quickly." Ikiso did that and the chicken ran inside the kitchen and went under her bed. She followed it there and caught it. She was breathing hard and sweating. The chicken was also panting, its eyes blinking with weariness.

"Father, I have caught it," Ikiso announced.

"Didn't I tell you?" Okanya said, coming out. "When you run after chicken spitting, it tires quickly. All right, bring it here, then get a knife and hot water." He went behind the house and Ikiso brought hot water and the knife and put them down quickly and went to the bush to get some leaves. She hated seeing anything being slaughtered. Once, at her uncle's place, she was called to hold one leg of a goat which was going to be slaughtered, with others holding the rest of it down. She had refused and cried. Her uncle had become angry with her. "Don't you want meat?" he had shouted at her. Of course she wanted meat but she could not bear to see the goat dying. She was thinking of all this while she was getting the leaves. She came back carrying them and took them to the kitchen. Her father was there, holding the dead chicken over the fire to burn off any hairs which remained. Ikiso put down the leaves then Okanya laid the chicken on them. Ikiso sat down and started her usual job of holding while her father sliced it methodically. Okanya washed his hands and told her to put it on the fire. "You can roast the liver and eat it if you want." Ikiso washed the meat and put it on the fire then she roasted the liver but she did not eat it. She took it to her sister. She sat down silently near her and presented her with the liver on a small white plate.

"Dear me!" Anaro exclaimed, "why don't you eat it?"

"But I want you to eat it," Ikiso said smiling.

"Ikiso is missing you a lot," their mother said. "The day you were taken, I found her asleep on our bed with traces of tears on her face."

"My dear, so you love me that much?"

132

"Of course," Ikiso answered, looking away. Her eyes were glittering with unshed tears. She hated to be pitied!

"How is Lilly?" Anaro asked.

"We hear that she is at the home of Okwapa but Okwapa is not at home."

"We hear that he had joined the army," Okanya said.

"Are you not going to eat the liver?" Ikiso asked and then smiled.

"I am going to eat it. Why are you smiling?"

"I am happy and I am remembering the last fight we had. Do you remember that day? The day you would not let us eat early?"

"I am sure there were so many of those days," Abeso put in.

"I mean the day you almost pushed me into the fire. I was trying to roast a potato since you had refused to serve the food."

"Oh that day!" Anaro said. "You knew I had cut my toe and my temper was short and there you were wanting to eat lunch at ten in the morning."

"Really it wasn't ten at all. Mother wouldn't have found me still crying."

"But that was what you used to do. Whenever we fought and you were defeated, as you usually were, you would want to cry until mother came back from wherever she had gone. Now it will be your turn to discipline someone," Anaro said shyly. Ikiso understood and dropped her eyes.

"I will not do what you used to do to me," Ikiso said.

Anaro untied the small bundle she had carried and then said, "Kampala people sent you these things." She produced two bars of key soap, three kilograms of sugar, two kilograms of salt and one packet of tea leaves. Putting her hand inside her dress, she got out a handkerchief which she untied saying, "And he gave you this, father, for cigarettes." She gave Okanya fifty shillings. "And this is for you, mother," she added, giving Abeso fifty shillings also.

"Thank you, thank you very much," they both said.

"Ikiso, take all these things to our bedroom," Abeso said.

"Thank him when you go back," Okanya said. "Where do you stay in Kampala?"

"We stay at Wandegeya Police barracks. Ewiu works there," Anaro answered. "Ah, but, father, Kampala is so big!"

"How big?"

"I think from here to Kalaki."

"Buildings all along?"

"Buildings all along. Some of them offices, others shops and others houses where people live. Most of the houses are *gorofa* houses."

"What is a *gorofa*?" Ikiso asked.

"A house on top of another house and so that many houses can pile up, isn't that so, Anna?" Okanya said.

"Yes, they are called storeyed."

"But can't the top house fall on top of those down?" Ikiso asked.

Okanya laughed. "No, my daughter. When you are inside a *gorofa* house, you can't even know you are up until you look through the window."

"How do you get there?" Ikiso asked inquisitively.

"There are steps," Anaro answered. "And there are things they call 'lifts'. A lift is just a small house without any windows but with a light in it. There is a man who operates the lift. You tell him the number and he presses it for you. The lift doors open and close by themselves and when you are inside, you feel being lifted. When it reaches the pressed number of the *gorofa*, the door again opens by itself and closes after you come out. You find yourself on the verandah of the *gorofa* you had asked for."

"Oh!" Ikiso said and both her parents laughed.

"You see," Okanya said, "when you go to visit your sister, she will show it to you. Where did you see the lift?" Okanya asked, looking at Anaro.

"Ewiu tells me that all the tall buildings in town have got that thing but I sat in one when we had gone to New Mulago Hospital. We had taken food to the wife of Ewiu's friend. She had given birth and she was in *gorofa* number five." Abeso and Ikiso were looking at Anaro eagerly, expecting her to say more

"Mulago Hospital," Okanya meditated." I hear it is very big."

"So big, father, that it has a bank, a post office and a police station all inside."

"Ah!" Okanya marvelled. "Europeans can do great things. Which *gorofa* did you see again?"

"He took me to the International Hotel and I don't know how to tell you how big it is. Ewiu said it has fifteen *gorofas*!"

"Ah," Ikiso said. "It must be very tall."

"Yes, it is so tall that people down look like insects to people up on the last *gorofa!* Ewiu wanted us to sit in the lift and be taken to the top but I refused. I hate lifts. You see, when it is lifting you, you feel as if your heart 'is going.' "

"Ikiso, go and see to the fire and bring us hot water," their mother said presently.

Okanya was shaking his head. "What about markets?" he asked.

"Markets are everywhere. Wandegeya has its own, Mulago, Kamwokya, and so on. But the main market is in the city. It is called Owino market. He took me there once. The distance is like from here to Lwala Mission but we used a bus.

"For such a short distance!" Okanya couldn't believe it.

"Yes, it seems people there don't walk because they are always standing at bus stages, waiting for buses."

"Are the buses many?" Abeso asked.

"There are very many buses, mother, lorries, and small cars, but few bicycles."

"Tell us about the market," Abeso said as Ikiso entered with hot water."What sort of things do they sell?"

"Oh, they sell all sorts of things, beans simsim, potatoes, tomatoes, green vegetables, fresh and dry fish, and so on."

"Drink, my daughter," Okanya said, handing her the tube. You are doing a lot of talking and not enough drinking."

"I am drinking," Anaro said, getting the tube and sucking.

"What about their churches?" Ikiso asked.

"Like markets, there are also very many churches for Christians and mosques for Moslems."

"What about at night?" Abeso asked at length. "We hear that you can pick a needle on the ground at night." To Ikiso, she said, "Go and see about food. It should be ready now. Your sister must be hungry."

"Mother, it is true," Anaro answered after sometime. "There is electricity everywhere. Along roads and in houses."

135

"What about water?"

"Mother, water is in the house. Our house is only two-roomed; a sitting room and a bedroom. Then there is a bathroom and a toilet within the house and a kitchen. There is water in the kitchen and bathroom. I tell you, mother, there is nothing I do there. I just cook, clean the house and wash clothes. Moreover, I can't iron his uniforms, he uses starch on them."

"Daniery," Abeso called her husband as though he was not there. "Anna says that Ewiu is a corporal."

"Is that so?" Okanya remarked. "It is a high rank in the police." Abeso looked tenderly at him because he knew so much she didn't know.

"Excuse me," Anaro said and left the room. She went to the kitchen and found Ikiso warming the food. She had already mingled millet bread.

"Ay, Ikiso, I see you are still sleeping here. Don't you fear?" Anaro asked, roaming about, opening and peeping into pots to see what they contained.

"I don't fear," Ikiso answered. "Sometimes Ameso comes to spend some nights here. She is my best friend. When you left she slept here with me for one week."

"She is a good girl," Anaro agreed.

"Go back inside, food is ready and please tell mother to come." Anaro went to the toilet first before going back to the house.

"Mother, Ikiso is calling you," she said sitting down.

"Ah!" Okanya resumed. "It is good Ewiu is looking after you well. I can see that. Now I don't know when he will come to give us the cows."

"I think it will be soon which is why he sent me back here. His mother told me that she has already prepared the beer herself with wives of Ewiu's uncle. She said I should return tomorrow because on Monday I will be going with her to Kakeno to grind, bury and fry it. Then I think they will send a letter to Ewiu before it is put in water."

"That will be okay," Okanya said. "You see, I am now anxious about your mother. It is better she goes there when it is still small."

"Yes, father," she said, then more quietly, "Father, I wish we had a brother."

136

"That is it, my child. Someone to take my place when I am gone!"

"I will pray that it be so, but what had happened to mother? Had someone 'hidden her uterus'?" she asked, as she got up to prepare her father's table for eating.

"I don't know and I don't know why all this time I had not thought of consulting a witch doctor about her. She went to that nurse, Rose and she told me that the nurse said no one had 'hidden her uterus' but that the irregularities of her 'monthly sickness' was what was stopping her from conceiving."

"You mean they became regular?"

"She said they became regular when Nurse Rose gave her some European medicines to swallow."

"I see, but—"she wanted to say more but when she saw her mother entering with Ikiso carrying food, she stopped. Okanya moved to his table with his chair. Ikiso took the pot of beer and put it aside. She sat near her sister and their mother sat on a cowhide, in front of them. Ikiso shared the plate of vegetables with her mother. Anaro had a separate plate. All visitors ate alone. They prayed and then they started to eat. The chicken was oily and sweet.

"Ikiso," Okanya called, "I hope you didn't throw away my legs."

"No, father, they are there."

"I will eat them tomorrow," he said.

"What about supper, won't you eat supper today?" Abeso asked.

"With this beer you think I can eat again? This is going to be enough."

"Men knew how sweet the chicken was so they prevented women from eating it. They must have been greedy," Anaro said, her mouth full.

"It wasn't greed; it was the custom."

"It was a terrible custom: how was the custom broken?"

"Europeans broke it saying chicken was necessary for everybody, especially small children and pregnant women because it adds blood. So everybody, including women, started eating chicken."

"I thank that European with all my heart, knowing how sweet chicken is."

"Do you eat it in Kampala also?"

137

"Ah, there it is so expensive. No, I did not eat any chicken there."

"I am glad I slaughtered this one for you."

"Thank you, father," Anaro said and they continued to eat. Okanya was the first to finish eating. So after washing his hands he went out.

"You are still at it?" he said smiling when he came back to the house.

"Why should they hurry? Where are they going?" Abeso reproached him.

"I am just talking," Okanya said. "I know you women are slow. I talk with my children when I am still alive. When I go who will they talk to? Woman, let me talk to my children." Okanya was starting to get drunk. After sometime they too finished to eat.

"I wish it could be always like this," Ikiso said and started collecting the plates.

"Thank you for cooking, mother, that was a wonderful meal."

"We are glad you came." A pause then, "Ikiso, come here a bit." Ikiso came.

"Make sure there is enough water in the saucepan and put that beer away. It is not strong now, then get us a fresh pot. It is there in our bedroom. I feel so lazy," she continued, "especially when I am full like this. It is good I have Ikiso to help me, what would I do>"

"I know," Anaro agreed as though she had ever been pregnant. After a short time, Ikiso brought a fresh port of beer, then hot water which she poured in it and sat down to drink also. They had enjoyed the meal so much there was little room for beer. So they just took little while Okanya drank steadily.

"Ah, daughter, tell me, did you drink again when you left here? I mean the day you were taken from here."

"Yes, there was a lot of beer there also."

"Ah! But the beer you brewed was so strong that after you had left, we drank until dawn. People ran away from beer; they just escaped without saying bye."

"Even there beer was much. Do you remember those boys who fought here? They resumed their quarrel and fought again. Ewiu's uncle then sent them away. The rest of the clan people, and even some *iwanyak,* drank until morning. They still remember that beer

and they praise you for the way eating and sitting was organised."
Okanya shook his head smiling, feeling good.

"Ikiso, you are drinking too much. Don't get drank," their mother
cautioned. "Have you seen our water pot? Remember, tomorrow is
Sunday."

"I am going with her, " Anaro said. "It is still hot."

Ikiso was so happy to hear that. "You are not changed a bit!" she
said. "I thought you were now a visitor?"

"Women are never visitors; come at mine and see if you won't
cook," Anarosaid teasingly.

"Yes, let us wait and see," Ikiso said happily. Anaro stayed with
her people until Sunday evening when she left.

Chapter Eighteen

It took Ebwonyu three weeks from the time Anaro came back from Kampala to be ready. So he sent Okanya a letter the day Ewiu came back, a Thursday, asking him to come with his clans people on the coming Saturday. Kakeno wasn't far from Ochuloi-Komua, so Okanya's people reached there at noon, after one hour's walk. They were welcomed and, given places to sit and then the ceremony started. The herdsman brought the cows to the compound, then Okanya and members of his group went to see the cows. With a stick, Ebwonyu beat gently the cows he was giving away. The fifteenth cow was rejected because it had only two nipples. "Show us another one," one member of Okanya's group said. "This one as you can see has only two nipples. It can't suckle its young well. Its calves will always be dying."

"I know," Ebwonyu replied, "but there is no other."

"What about all those cows?"

"Those, as you know, are my neighbours. We look after our cows together, in turns."

"Then in that case, when will we hope to get another one?" the same man persisted.

"I will try to get another one soon," Ebwonyu promised. The cows Ebwonyu had shown them were fat and healthy looking. So Okanya's people didn't press him too much for that last one. After that, the cows were taken back to graze and the people went back to the *goga* where food was immediately served with fresh goat's meat and different types of dry fish mixed with either simsim paste or pounded groundnuts. They ate but they could not finish the food. So after they had had enough, they washed their hands and then sat back and talked while removing pieces of meat from their teeth, using stems of grass. When the place was cleared, pots of beer were brought, tubes distributed and hot water poured. Then people started to drink. At first they talked quietly but as they continued to drink, they became louder. Cigarette smoke hung in the air like tiny scattered clouds. Lakeri, Ewiu's mother, called Abeso to a small room. "Let us sit here, my daughter," she said. They sat on a mat and they had a pot of beer in front of them. "My daughter," Lakeri said, "and now you are a friend. I am very glad it was your daughter my son decided to bring. Your daughter is a good girl."

"Thank you , Lakeri," Abeso said. "I am also glad it is you who is now going to be her mother."

"Now my friend," Lakeri said gently, "what is this I hear about you? Is it true?"

"What have you heard about me?"

"That you are going to 'see outside' (give birth) again after such a long pause."

"I still don't know the truth because I am just feeling fine and not vomiting. All my two daughters used to make me vomit every morning but since I stopped seeing my 'monthly sickness', I haven't vomited. That is why I tell you that I am not so sure." Lakeri listened attentively; observing Abeso.

Abeso had put on a *gomasi,* so it wansn't easy to see whether her abdomen was big or not. "That is not unusual," Lakeri said. "Because I vomited with all my ten girls who died and by the time I got Ewiu, I was so miserable, I thought that my misery of losing my children was the reason for my not vomiting, but it was not so. It was only a change in sex," she said.

"I am sorry," Abeso said. "I thought Ewiu was your only child."

"Yes, he is the only child now, but he had sisters who were all called to 'feed the earth'."

"I am sorry," Abeso repeated.

"It is all right, I don't worry about them anymore. After all, don't I have your daughter now?"

"That is okay."

"This world is like that, we are never sure of anything," Lakeri said.

Outside the noise was now a din. People were singing and dancing. So they listened to the song which Okanya's people were singing and dancing to. They sang:

AⅡ - *Awotin ber, Awotin ber*
- *Kono Mam Ewiu ya kono Okwia kop me jo Kakeno*
- *Wan wele, wele Ewiu*
- *Wan wele, wele Ewiu, Echuloit me onong o-o-o!*

They sang in turns, men with big voices first, then women in small voices next, again and again until they were tired.

"That is a very nice song," Lakeri said.

"Yes, it is good to have friends. Do you think I have forgotten how you helped me with Okanya?"

"That is all right, my friend. How is he now?"

"He is all right but the other day he told me that when he gets these cows he will marry another woman."

"He will not do it since you are now pregnant."

They chatted for a long time. Anaro came in from time to time to refresh their drink and to bring hot water. They drank so much that whole day, night and morning. They left in the afternoon of Sunday. Okanya and Abeso were praised for producing Anaro. Everyone was happy except Orace as usual. He took his complaints to Esemu. "I told you this man has charms," he said. Esemu kept quiet. "Did you see the cows?" Orace went on. "Such fat, healthy cows! How could Ebwonyu show such cows if this man hadn't tricked him with his charms?"

Esemu became annoyed and irritated. "Why do you always talk of Okanya like that? Okanya is a good man."

"See?" Orace said. "He has got you too."

"Never talk to me about Okanya again, Orace, or I will tell him. It is you always talking about Okanya and abusing him that he has no son,

142

yet I have been with Okanya many times but not once did he mention your name or refer to that fight you had at my place. Orace, why do you hate Okanya so much?"

"I don't hate him," Orace replied sadly.

"Then why are you always trying to spoil his name? I know you Orace, you are just jealous!" Esemu said. He was fed up with Orace's attitude towards Okanya. He had spoken harshly to Orace, so after that they walked home in silence.

Two weeks later the cows for Anaro's dowry were brought to Okanya's home. He had built a small kraal for them with the help of his friend, Esemu. The day the cows were brought people again ate and drank but Orace was not among them. "What has happened to Orace?" Okanya asked, after coming back from saying goodbye to the boys of Kakeno who had brought cows. "Yet I invited him."

Esemu said quietly, "You, Okanya, are my friend. I know that you have ever kept so many secretes of mine, that is why I am now going to tell you this." He stopped dramatically, got the tube and sucked for a long time. Okanya was puzzled but he sat and waited. "We have been friends for a long time," Esemu continued, "so I know you. I am going to tell you about Orace."

"Yes?" Okanya prompted him, sitting forward.

"Orace thinks you have got a powerful charm and that is why everything is always going right for you."

"Is that so? I think Orace is just stupid. How can he say a thing like that! In any case, God has been more kind to him. He has been given sons and daughters but what about me, Okanya? Who will look after this compound when I amgone? If I were to die now, wouldn't it just collapse? He is just laughing at me as always, let him go ahead. When he dies his name will remain behind but what about poor me? What about me?" Okanya felt so bad, he supported his head in his hands, crushed with misery. Hatred for Orace went through him, making his head pound and his eyes darken with rage! "Why doesn't he leave me alone? He has everything, yes, but when have I ever asked for his sons? Do I eat noonday meals at his home?" Okanya was furious.

"I am sorry," Esemu said. "I did not want to tell you this but Orace has been disturbing me a lot about that. In fact he started his talks when Ewiu came to ask for your daughter. I have been bearing that man but the other day when we were coming back from Kakeno, he came again to me with his usual complaints, I became very irritated with him and I told him that he was just feeling jealous. Then I warned him that I would tell you. I think he thought I had already told you about it, that is why he didn't come."

"I see."

"Now, my friend, I ask you to behave to him as though you don't know anything. It is foolish to show your annoyance."

"Thank you, my friend," Okanya said. "You have made me know my enemy. The one man I fed more than even you, my friend."

When everyone had gone, Okanya told Abeso what Esemu had told him and she also reported the conversation she had overheard between Esemu and Orace, the day Ewiu and his people had come to ask for their daughter in marriage.

"It is good when one knows one's enemy," Okanya said.

"Yet the way I had cooked for that man!" Abeso lamented.

Chapter Nineteen

A month after the cows were brought, Anaro came to her parents to say goodbye after which she left for Kampala. Ikiso continued reading hard since primary leaving examinations were to be held soon, in November. Abeso's pregnancy continued to grow and she continued to visit the hospital as advised by Nurse Rose. In December Okanya gathered in his cotton and sold it. He got 300/= which to him was a lot of money. He bought his wife and daughter dresses and bought himself a new pair of trousers and a shirt.

The following year, 1964, was the happiest in Okanya's life. First, his daughter Ikiso passed in grade 'A'. She was admitted at Namagunga St. Mary's Secondary school. This piece of good news came early in January, 1964. In February the same year, Okanya's two cows gave birth to healthy calves. It meant that these cows were brought from Ebwonyu's place when they were already pregnant. Before Okanya could recover from these happy events, in March his wife gave birth to the long longed-for son! This time surely he would celebrate! So four days after Abeso was discharged from the hospital, the birth of the small boy was celebrated.

Three days before that, Awao, Okanya's brother's wife, went round the village inviting men and women of the clan only, to come to 'bring Abeso out'. So the young visitor since leaving hospital did not see the sun until the fourth day. On that day, all women came very early, carrying pots of water and after greeting the mother and child, they divided themselves into groups. One group went to look for firewood, another got millet out of the granary, threshed it and ground it. Another group, usually the senior wives, went out in the bush to get different types of herbs for bathing the small boy. By ten o'clock, everything was ready; that is the firewood, the millet and the water which was on fire to boil for drinking. Awao had brewed for the occasion at Abeso's house. Awao also smeared cowdung over the floors of Abeso's big house and kitchen and swept the compound clean. Soon after, men started to arrive. This time, Orace came too, because Okanya continued to treat him as though nothing had happened. Of course Orace was very envious and now firmly convinced that Okanya had something. First Okanya's cotton had done well; his daughter was now safely in one of the best schools in Uganda and now a son, a buried hope for so many years!

The old women pounded some herbs and chewed the bark of *ebyong* tree; then they made small ropes which they tied round the mother's and baby's necks, waists, wrists and ankles. They then caught the baby by the legs and turned him upside down and put his head in the mortar where the herbs were already mixed with water. This took only a minute before they put him down. While all this was being done, the baby kept on crying and kicking and when the ceremony was over, he was given back to his mother, who wrapped him up in clothes and fed him. All this was done inside the house. The men sat outside smoking and talking about different things. The women then started drinking *cet a tin* (faeces of the baby) beer from a very tiny pot. They drank *cet a tin* and ate the residue. After that, the men and women were then given a big pot of beer each. Meanwhile, the women continued carrying the baby in turns. "Bring him here," Agenesi said. "By the way, what is his name?"

"His father wants him to be called after him."

"Is that so?" The women were all surprised because that was unusual. A man always named his children after his parents and relatives.

"Well," Abeso said "that is what he calls him."

"Okay," Orace's wife said. "Bring my husband here." When the child was given to her, she talked to the child endlessly. "My husband, where have you been hiding? You finished tears from our eyes and

146

you dried the left ones from our hearts. You must now grow quickly so that you can build your wife a house and grow a lot of cotton to buy her dresses. Do you hear?" The baby just looked around innocently, grabbing endlessly at what others could not see. Agenesi made a tiny shield, using leaves and got a small dry grass to represent the spear. Then she forced open the baby's left hand and put the shield in it and then the right hand was also forced open and the little spear was put in it after which he was left alone. He waved the shield and the spear and dropped them, at which the women laughed and clapped.

"Good, good, our man. You must grow to be a warrior and defend us from the Karamojong raiders," Orace's wife said and everyone laughed. After that the baby fell asleep and he was taken to the inner room and put to bed.

Meanwhile, the men were starting to get drunk. One could tell from the raised voices and the repetitious stories. They drank until late. All left except Esemu and Orace. Orace was in a good mood that day and talked a lot. Then afterwards he lowered his voice and said, "Okanya, I would like to ask you a certain question which I have kept in my chest for a long time. In fact, I think it has stayed there now for one year."

"Yes?" Okanya asked.

"I would like to ask when we are two."

"Okay," Esemu said and got up. "I can go."

"No," Okanya said, holding Esemu down to his chair. "We are all brothers and friends, Orace, is that not so?" he asked.

"It is so," Orace answered.

"Then why can't you speak in Esemu's presence?"

"Because it is a secret."

"There is no secret between me and Esemu," Okanya said.

"Actually," Orace stated," I am asking you to help me too." On hearing that, Esemu guessed what was coming so he kept his ears open but pretended to concentrate on his drinking tube.

"Help you in what way?" Okanya asked.

"You see, I have been through bad times throughout," he said and kept quiet, looking down.

"Well?" Okanya prompted him.

"Even if it means giving you some money or even a goat, I can do it," Orace went on. Okanya was getting tired of this type of talk, and couldn't even guess what was about to be said, so he started drinking. "I mean," Orace found it very difficult to say what he wanted to say. It was a delicate matter. "Well," he continued, "according to how I see it, it seems you have some powerful charm that makes everything go right for you. So I am begging you to divide it and give me a little too."

Okanya sat upright and stopped drinking and laughed a little. "Me, Orace?" he said. "What makes you think like that?" Esemu was now alert, ears and eyes open, looking at Orace.

"Well, as I said, things just go well with you. See your cotton last year, your daughter now in the best school and out of nowhere, your wife—" he could not finish the sentence. Okanya just shook his head. He could not help feeling triumphant over Orace, since Orace was always tormenting him about a son. Now he had a son, may God keep him. He felt so pleased seeing Orace looking miserable.

"Well," he said smiling, "I have nothing at all, Mr Orace, except that probably I was just born lucky. That is all. Now, gentleman, if you will forgive me please, we can call it a day. Mr Esemu, I will see you tomorrow." He bade them goodbye and they left. "I was just born lucky," he repeated after the retreating miserable back of Orace